With

With the ⸻⸻⸻ ⸻ ⸻⸻⸻, Cassie ⸻⸻⸻
on Raul. "How dare you!"

"Please calm down, *patrona*," Raul said, raising both
hands in a peace-making gesture. "I was only trying to
help."

"Help?" She punched at his chest with her pointer
finger. "I ordered you to let Jesse go. Now you've only
managed to make things worse. You know who that was?"

Beneath his drooping, walrus mustache, Raul pursed
his lips and spat on the ground. "I am not afraid of that
pistolero."

"You don't say?" Cassie put her hands on her hips.
"So you had everything under control until I showed up,
right?"

"I did not know the boy was with him," Raul said
with a shrug. "I only wished t-"

"Enough!" She stopped him with a wave of her hand.
"If you hadn't interfered, none of this would've happened."

Retrieving her gun, Cassie holstered it securely. Her
angry gaze settled on Paco and Mario standing by the
barn, actively exchanging glances.

"Leave us," she said to them. "I'll deal with you two
later."

The brothers darted by her amid a flurry of
awkwardly mumbled apologies.

Raul walked up behind her. "Do not punish them,
patrona. They were only doing as I ordered."

"I know they were," Cassie said, rounding on him,
"that's the problem. You seem to forget that *I* am boss
here."

"I do not forget." He pulled his shoulders back and
stood tall. "I only wish to help, like I helped Don Garrett
for so many years."

Cassie swallowed the acrid lump in her throat. He
always played this card with her.

Dry Moon

by

Karyna Da Rosa

Dry Moon

Contact Information: info@thewildrosepress.com

Cover Art by *Dawn Seewer* - www.dagiandesigns.com

The Wild Rose Press
PO Box 706
Adams Basin, NY 14410-0706
Visit us at www.thewildrosepress.com

Publishing History
First Cactus Rose Edition, January 2007
Print ISBN 1-60154-035-3

Published in the United States of America

Dedication

To my very first reading group, fan club, and personal
motivators: Alina, Monica, Meagan, and of course,
Jennifer.

Chapter 1

"Look, *señorita*." Raul Villanueva braced a large, bear-like hand on the boy's shoulder and forced him to his knees. "I found him sneaking around the reservoir."

Frowning, Cassie Taylor gazed into a pair of familiar, glacier-blue eyes. "That's Jesse Pruitt." She looked at her range boss, eliciting a grunt of acknowledgement from the stocky man. "Isn't he working for Barrington now?"

"*Si, patrona*," Raul said, using the Spanish term for "boss-lady" as was customary of the ranch hands when addressing her, "and it looks like he is doing Barrington's dirty work, too."

"What were you doing out there, Jesse?" Cassie asked the young intruder. She tucked her brown slicker behind her gun belt and revealed the single-action .44 Schofield holstered at her hip.

With a nervous glance directed at the exposed weapon, the boy swallowed hard. His chin quivered, and he ducked his head to stare at the ground, a mass of blond curls tumbled around his shoulders. Cassie reckoned he was anywhere between twelve and fourteen years of age, though she doubted even Jesse knew for sure.

"Well," she asked amid his continued silence, "you got anything to say for yourself?"

"*Patrona*, you leave him to me, *si*? I know how to make this one talk." Raul lifted Jesse by his shirt collar.

"No, I'll handle this," Cassie said. "Fetch me Paco and Mario. Then get back to work."

Raul glowered at her through narrowed eyes, a tacit challenge simmered in their obsidian depths. Pressing his lips into a bloodless line, he marched by her, grunting an expletive Cassie deemed best to ignore.

"Nobody's gonna hurt you," she said to Jesse, in a softer tone. "Just tell me what you were doing out there."

The boy continued to stare at the ground. "N-nothin'."

1

From behind her, the sound of jangling spurs drew Cassie's attention. She turned, eyeing the two men approaching her. Mario, short, rotund, and painfully shy, ducked his coffee-colored eyes the moment they met hers, a deep blush rose from his neck to stain his cherubic face. Paco, a year older than his brother, Mario, gave her an acknowledging grin. The pole opposite of Mario in every way, he was tall and slender, but there was strength in the ample breadth of his shoulders, self-assurance in his stance. With features carved from stone, he looked older than his twenty-two years.

"You called for us, *patrona*?" Paco asked.

"Escort Jesse here to the gates," she ordered. "Make sure he leaves."

Paco cut a scathing look at the golden-hair trespasser. "*Andale, gringo!*"

Jesse was quick to comply. He hurried along the rocky path, flanked by the disparate pair of brothers. Cassie watched the trio disappear around the bend, and then took a deep breath, her lungs swelled with the gritty afternoon air. Striding back to her house, she smiled at the woman standing on the covered front porch, holding the wooden, mesh door open.

"Is everything okay, *señorita*?"

Cassie looked at her housekeeper and trusted confidant. "Not really, Juanita."

"Come," Juanita said with a wave of her hand, "I have something that will cheer you up, *si*?"

Trailing Juanita into the kitchen, Cassie inhaled the sweetly mingled aromas of freshly brewed coffee and her favorite, apricot fritters.

"Mmm..." she purred, taking a seat at the rectangular, wooden table. Her gaze flitted from the potbelly stove to the wooden cupboards, in search of the delectable treats.

Smiling, Juanita shook her head, her thick braid swinging like an onyx pendulum across her back. "They were for dessert tonight," she said, scooping the plate of fritters, obscured behind the lace-trimmed curtains, from the kitchen window. "But I think we can enjoy them now."

Watching Juanita set the fritters on the tabletop, Cassie rubbed her hands with unabashed relish. "Now's a good a time as any," she agreed, wasting no time digging into the warm, flaky pie. "Honestly, Juanita," she mouthed between bites, "every time you make these, they seem to taste even better."

At the potbelly stove, Juanita poured two cups of coffee. She returned to the table and handed one to Cassie. "I am glad you like them, *señorita*," she said, taking a seat beside her. "I do not like to see you upset."

Cassie licked apricot jam from her fingers. "I'm not upset, Juanita. Just worried, is all."

"What was the boy doing?" Juanita asked.

"He wouldn't say, but I reckon checking on the water level."

Juanita's brown, acorn-shaped eyes flared with indignation. "Barrington again?"

"Who else?" Cassie said, pursing her mouth with distaste. "None of the other ranchers are this much trouble, except for Amos. He's convinced I'm bilking him on his share of the water, and Jesse works for him now."

"Barrington is *el Diablo* himself!" Juanita's tone was pure venom.

"Worse than the Devil," Cassie said, taking a sip of her coffee. "But this drought ain't making things any easier. Another month without rain and I'll have to start rationing everyone's share."

"That will only make Barrington angrier."

Cassie nodded. "I know. I'm not looking forward to making that announcement at the next meeting. But I don-" The sound of a single gunshot outside severed her words.

With a startled gasp, Juanita dropped her cup on the floor. Cassie sprang to her feet, drawing her weapon.

"No matter what happens, stay inside, Juanita," she demanded, stepping over the porcelain fragments.

"*Si, señorita*," Juanita said in a tremulous voice.

Cassie sprinted outside, just as the sound of another gunshot pierced the still air. It came from the side of the barn, and she followed it, skidding to a sudden halt when she encountered a man on horseback. With a gun in each hand aimed at her men, the stranger appeared to have gotten the better of Raul, Paco, and Mario. On the ground, well out of reach, were the trio's gun belts. The weaponless men stood with arms raised in surrender.

Cassie surveyed the formidable stranger, feeling a tight knot constrict her throat. He was tall, six feet two or three she reckoned, judging by the length of those denim clad legs flanking the sides of his copper bay horse. Though lean as a rattler, he was powerfully built, with broad shoulders and strong, muscle-lined forearms, visible by the white sleeves rolled up to his elbows. Beneath his Stetson, dark eyes brimming with contempt scoured the length of her.

"You better have a mighty good reason for being on my property, mister," she said, the staunch tone of her voice belying her inner trepidation.

"Be careful, *patrona*," she heard Raul whisper, prompting her to glance his way.

It was then she saw Jesse.

Her stomach lurched. The taste of soured apricots filled her mouth at the sight of the boy on his knees beside Raul. From the looks of him, she doubted he was even conscious. Blood matted his golden hair against his right cheek, and one eye was swollen shut. Another thin ribbon of blood trickled down the side of his mouth, staining his white shirt. She glared accusingly at Raul, who plucked his chin upward in a show of mute defiance.

Damn him.

"I'm just here for the kid, ma'am," the armed rider said. His tone was cool, almost conversational. "Don't want no trouble."

Looking at the stranger, Cassie spoke to Raul over her shoulder. "Stay put and don't do anything stupid."

She took a few cautionary steps toward the gunman, stopping only when he pointed one of his weapons at her. A double-action .45 Colt Lightening. Her mouth went dry as a desert arroyo. The gun was favored by professional gunfighters.

"That's close enough," he warned.

Her blood raced, thundered like a galloping stallion in her ears, as she gazed into that long, nickel silver barrel.

She tossed her shoulders back. "This boy was trespassing."

"So you're having him beaten to death?" he said,

4

glaring at her.

His words stung like a slap across her face, but she wasn't about to explain herself to this surly stranger. Let him think her ruthless.

"This here's private property, mister. What happens here is no concern of yours. Now, you're free to leave," she said, cocking the hammer of her revolver for emphasis, "or I can have the undertaker fetch you. Your choice."

The threat seemed to have negligible, if any, effect on the stranger. "And here I thought you were the smart one of the bunch," he said, with a lazy, insolent grin.

"Shoot him, *patrona*!" Raul shouted suddenly.

The outburst startled Cassie, but she managed to keep her gun steady despite her slick grip. Cursing, she slid a warning look Raul's way.

It was all the opening the gunman needed. Like a striking diamondback, he kicked her outstretched hand, and her weapon spiraled to the ground. Before she could react, the man was off his mount, wrestling her arm behind her back. Cassie's shoulder socket ignited with a searing pain as her captor forced her hand higher between her shoulder blades.

"Some firepower you're packin', darlin'," he remarked. "Sure you know how to use it?"

"Do not harm her!" Raul yelled. "I will give you the boy, just let her go."

"Now that's mighty obliging of you," the man drawled. "How's about you get Jesse into my saddle there, and I'll hand this pretty gal over."

Raul remained immobile, pensively stroking his bearded jaw as if mulling over his options.

From behind her, Cassie heard the gunman mutter a few choice expletives. "Call off the dogs, *Miss Taylor*," he ordered, inching her hand even higher, "or I'll have you hogtied and whipped once I'm through with them."

Another sickening jolt of white-hot pain spiked through Cassie's arm. "Don't recollect us meeting before," she managed through clenched teeth. "Who are you?"

Her answer was a rough, tooth-jarring shake. "Quit stallin' and do it!"

"Take Jesse to his horse," Cassie finally shouted to Raul. "Now!"

With a snarl, Raul reached for the battered boy, who wobbled on his feet like a newborn foal as the stronger man dragged him to the waiting mount.

"Atta girl," the stranger whispered. His lips brushed the sensitive skin behind Cassie's ear.

A tingling sensation skidded along her neck like an icy serpent. "Next time we run into each other," Cassie hissed, "it'll be *your* head at the end of my gun."

"Now, darlin', ya just met me and already you're itchin' to see me again," he said, pulling her tight against the steel length of his body.

Cassie squirmed in protest to no avail. The man's hold on her was simply unbreakable, and she only managed to cause more pain to her already throbbing arm. Without warning, her captor shoved her away. Cassie landed on her hands and knees, dust billowing around her in a granular cloud. From her peripheral vision, she saw Raul running toward her, his brawny arms extended as if to help her rise. Then he stopped and stared at something behind her, his ruddy face visibly paling.

Following his line of vision, Cassie turned to find the gunman standing over her, a dark, foreboding sentinel with a gun at her head.

"You have the boy, *si*? Now you go," Raul said.

"The sooner you join your amigos there," the man said, indicating Paco and Mario with a jerk of his head, "the sooner I'll head on out."

"Go on, Raul," Cassie ordered.

With a terse nod, Raul backed away.

Cassie glowered at the gunman as he dropped to one knee, putting himself at her eye level. Her stomach clenched like a tight fist as his unexpectedly handsome face came into clear view for the first time.

"Next time I see you," he warned, his voice like gravel, "I'll give you the same courtesy you extended Jesse."

Cassie lifted her chin, her injured pride fueling her limp tongue. "Reckon he'll think twice before trespassin' again."

A muscle twitched along the hard, sculpted line of his jaw, and he reached for her, wrapping a strong hand around her neck. "You're lucky you ain't but a female," he said, discarding her forcefully, as if she sullied him somehow.

Rubbing her sore neck, Cassie cursed the insufferable man as he leisurely stroll to his horse as if he didn't have a care in the world. He climbed into the saddle behind Jesse, who slumped against his chest with an audible sigh.

Kneeing his mount to circle Cassie the stranger said, "To answer your question, the name's Cole Mitchell." He gave her a cold, biting grin. "And for your sake, *darlin'*, you better pray we never meet again."

Chapter 2

With the ferocity of a caged animal, Cassie whirled on Raul. "How dare you!"

"Please calm down, *patrona*," Raul said, raising both hands in a peace-making gesture. "I was only trying to help."

"Help?" She punched at his chest with her pointer finger. "I ordered you to let Jesse go. Now you've only managed to make things worse. You know who that was?"

Beneath his drooping, walrus mustache, Raul pursed his lips and spat on the ground. "I am not afraid of that *pistolero*."

"You don't say?" Cassie put her hands on her hips. "So you had everything under control until I showed up, right?"

"I did not know the boy was with him," Raul said with a shrug. "I only wished t-"

"Enough!" She stopped him with a wave of her hand. "If you hadn't interfered, none of this would've happened."

Retrieving her gun, Cassie holstered it securely. Her angry gaze settled on Paco and Mario standing by the barn, actively exchanging glances.

"Leave us," she said to them. "I'll deal with you two later."

The brothers darted by her amid a flurry of awkwardly mumbled apologies.

Raul walked up behind her. "Do not punish them, *patrona*. They were only doing as I ordered."

"I know they were," Cassie said, rounding on him, "that's the problem. You seem to forget that *I* am boss here."

"I do not forget." He pulled his shoulders back and stood tall. "I only wish to help, like I helped Don Garrett for so many years."

Cassie swallowed the acrid lump in her throat. He

always played this card with her.

"You don't have to remind me about your years of service to my father, Raul. I remember them well," she said. "But that doesn't give you the right to run this outfit as you damn well please. After Pa passed on, he left me in charge, not you. So pay close attention, because I'm only going to say this once..." Cassie stared at the shorter man down the length of her nose, "...challenge my authority again, and I'll run you outta here like a mangy dog. Do I make myself clear?"

Scrunching his thick, black brows, Raul's face paled. "*Si, patrona*," he replied in a pained, thin voice, "very clear."

"Good. Now get out of my sight!"

With a departing nod, Raul disappeared toward the bunkhouse.

Muttering a curse, Cassie stalked along the serpentine path to the main entrance of her ranch. Both iron gates stood wide open. She stopped between them, her eyes scanning the rust-colored buttes peppering the horizon.

So that was Cole Mitchell. She finally had a face to put with the main topic of conversation in town for the past few weeks. Last she'd heard Barrington and his nemesis, Cyrus Miller, had some sort of bidding contest over the gunslinger. Of course the former, being the most affluent resident in the area, won out.

Staring into the vast, desert landscape, she wondered how far Mitchell managed to get. Barrington's Triple C Ranch was just over the next ridge, but carrying an injured rider was sure to slow him down. Her shoulders slumped with the weight of renewed remorse.

Poor Jesse.

A dry, painful knot swelled in her throat. Cassie swallowed hard, grimacing as it raked a burning trail to the pit of her stomach. Around her neck, the imprint of Mitchell's hand pulsated with a rhythmic beat, each digit a heated, throbbing brand. On impulse, she brought her hand to it, tracing the reddened marks she knew his fingers left behind.

****

Cole pulled Jesse upright, using one hand on the

reins and the other to cradle the unconscious boy in the crook of his arm. He shook his head, his thoughts reverting to Cassie Taylor. Reckon Barrington was right about her. She was one odd stick. Crazier than a loon, too. No woman in her right mind would go around wearing trousers and a gun belt, especially with a body like that. His mind shuffled through images of long, slender legs, shapely hips, and high, upswept breasts. Holding her against him, he realized she wasn't soft like most women. Instead, she was lean and firm, her body a sinewy twine of muscle. She was tall, too, a trait he'd never found particularly attractive in a female. But for some reason, it only added to this one's raw, sexual appeal. Just like those exotic, emerald eyes, wide and lifting in their corners, contrasting that thick mass of black, wavy hair. He clenched his jaw, chasing the unsettling thoughts away. One glance at Jesse was all it took to remind him that despite the angelic face, the woman was meaner than a biting boar.

Cole rode through the imposing, steel arched entrance of the Triple C, past Barrington's dual-story, adobe hacienda and stopped in the stables. Dismounting, he plucked Jesse off the saddle, using extra care to toss the boy over his shoulder.

As Cole strode to the bunkhouse, he saw Barrington emerge from the main house and hurry toward him. It took him a might longer than any ordinary man would. Barrel-chested, with a thick gut that rested far below his gun belt, the cattle baron's face had gone from crimson to a sickly purplish hue by the time he reached Cole.

"What the hell happened to him?" Barrington asked as he followed Cole into the bunkhouse.

"You did," Cole said, tenderly arranging Jesse's body on the narrow bed, hoping the kid remained unconscious while they tended to his wounds.

"Damn, just look at the poor bastard," Barrington muttered, his wet, blue eyes scanning the boy's limp form. He shook his head, tsking as he met Cole's eyes. "Good thing I sent you for him when I realized he was taking too long. Ain't that right?" he said with a nervous chuckle. "But don't worry none, Mitchell. I'll get Rosa. She'll fix him up good."

"Someone oughtta fix you good," Cole said, in a tone that implied he was seriously considering the prospect.

"Come now, man." Barrington slapped Cole's back in a friendly gesture. "I done nothing but take good care of that boy. Curly Pete treated that flea-bitten mutt of his better than Jesse, his own kin, mind you. Why, he had him scrubbing the floors of that saloon, wouldn't even feed him proper. But I gave him a good-paying job, a warm bed to sleep in, too."

"You fetchin' Rosa, or you want me to do that, too?" Cole asked with palpable irritation.

"Well, of course I am," Barrington said in a fluster. With a scowl, he opened the bunkhouse door and shouted, "Raines!"

Not a moment passed before Ike Raines, range boss of the Triple C, sauntered into the bunkhouse. Tall and wiry, with stringy, wheat-colored hair that brushed the high collar of his chambray shirt, he had the look of one who was always up to no good. He leaned against the wall, gray eyes darting a glance between Cole and the unconscious Jesse. The corner of his narrow mouth twitched, as if he fought back a smile. Cole tensed, clenched his fists. If the bastard laughed, he'd knock his teeth in.

Keeping an insolent eye on Cole, Raines addressed Barrington. "Yeah, boss?"

"Get the healer. Have her take care of the kid."

Raines spat a slick wad of tobacco juice on the wooden floor. "Sure thing, boss," he replied, winking at Cole before exiting the room.

"You see," Barrington's voice took on a more conciliatory tone, "Rosa's gonna take good care of him." He opened the door. "Let's go to the main house," he said, signaling Cole to follow. "There's something I wanna discuss with you in private."

Cole trailed the cattle baron outside with some reluctance. He kept glancing over his shoulder until he saw Rosa's heavyset figure ambling toward the bunkhouse. He let out a deep breath, knowing Jesse couldn't be in better hands.

Inside the hacienda, Barrington's wife, Katherine, greeted both men in the sitting room.

11

"Amos, I wasn't expecting company," she said, her voice soft and lyrical.

She was a classical beauty, with golden hair, porcelain skin, and large, hazel eyes. Her figure, though a bit too much on the slender side for Cole's liking, was perfectly proportioned. She was a lot younger than Barrington, too. Closer to his own age, Cole surmised. And it was plain as the hump on a camel that money was the only thing keeping a gal like that at Barrington's side.

Katherine's golden gaze shifted between her husband and Cole. "Amos, would you like me to prepare some coffee?" she asked, her eyes lingering on Cole.

"No," Barrington said. "We'll be in the library, and I don't want to be disturbed."

"Of course," Katherine answered.

Cole tipped his hat at her. "Ma'am," he saluted, feeling the habitual weight of her eyes on his back.

It unsettled him, the way she always watched him, those golden eyes sharp, brilliant with a keen awareness that belied her coy demeanor. He wondered if Barrington ever saw beyond the pretty face, ever managed to probe that ingenuous, bright-eyed gaze to the shrewd, darker core.

"Come in man, don't just stand there," Barrington said, ushering Cole through the library doors.

Cole stepped inside, admiring the lush surroundings. No one could accuse Barrington's wife of bad taste, that's for sure. The woodwork in the library alone probably cost a fortune. Heavy oak case molding trimmed the perimeter of the brick colored walls. The oversized mahogany desk in the center of the room gleamed with a fresh coat of polishing oil, as did the floor-to-ceiling bookshelves lining the walls on opposite sides.

Cole took one of the two leather seats across the desk, sinking into the plush cushion. He watched as Barrington rummaged through a small, wooden bar in the corner of the room. With a crystal tumbler wedged below each beefy arm, the big man held a bottle of whiskey high in the air, offering him a drink, which Cole declined.

With a shrug and a roll of his eyes that implied 'your loss' Barrington sat in his chair and filled his own glass. He guzzled the amber contents, propped his gleaming, black leather boots on the desk and proceeded to light a cigar.

Cole had met all sorts of men in his twenty-odd years of existence. Had done all kinds of morally ambiguous jobs, too. He'd cavorted with the most unsavory criminals west of the Mississippi. Every job was just that-a job. Cole kept his emotions separate from his profession. In his line of work, a man simply had to. Yet, there was something about Barrington that sickened him. And try as he might, Cole couldn't seem to quell his aversion of the cattle baron. It wasn't the man's piggish appearance, per say. *Though the only thing more bloated than the man's gut was his ego.* He had never met a more overbearing, egotistical, puffed up individual before. But still, there was something else. Something intangible, something on the inside that was just *off* about the man. *Maybe he should've taken the job with that Miller feller...*

"Here," Barrington said, producing a thick stack of hundred dollar banknotes, cinched with a leather band. "A little bonus for fetchin' the boy," he explained with a smug grin. "You're my main man here now. I don't want no hard feelings."

Anger coiled in Cole's belly like a burning whip. He pushed the notes away and leaned forward. "You can take your money and stick it where the sun don't shine. I don't do this kind of dirty work. You seen what they did to Jesse?"

Between gauzy strands of smoke, Barrington eyed him pensively and refilled his glass. "Look Mitchell, I only sent the kid to check on the water levels. How was I supposed to know that crazy tramp would skin his hide for that?"

"Why can't you leave well enough alone?" Cole said with disgust. "You're gettin' your fair share of the water."

"It ain't enough!" Barrington bellowed, pounding a meaty fist on the desktop. "I own more stock in Taylor Irrigation than any of the other members, so I should get more water than the others. I got more land to irrigate and more livestock than anybody in this blasted town."

"You can bellyache all you want, Amos," Cole cut in. "Don't change the fact that the Taylor woman owns all the water rights and the irrigation company. Like it or not,"

13

he snorted, knowing his words would hit a sore spot, "she's the big bug in this hellhole of a town, not you."

Barrington gave Cole an irascible look over the rim of his tumbler and drained the contents in one greedy gulp. "So, finally got to meet her, did ya?" he asked, setting the empty glass on the desktop. He emitted a wet belch and wiped his mouth with the back of one crisp, starched sleeve. "She's quite a woman, ain't she?"

The lascivious undertone in Barrington's voice unsettled him. Cole shifted uncomfortably in his seat. "Reckon some men would think so."

"Yeah," Barrington said with a knowing wink. "I prefer me a more delicate type, myself. Takes a steeple-jack to look that woman in the eye!" He leaned forward, resting his beefy forearms on his desk, dropping his voice as if he were about to divulge a sordid secret. "You know her ma was a Mexican whore?"

Cole shrugged. "So?"

Barrington puckered his face with distaste. "Can't trust no Mexican. Especially a woman. Though she looks white, don't she? She favored Garrett," he reflected thoughtfully. "That son of a bitch cut quite a swell with the ladies. But she took after her ma in other ways. Runs that outfit flat on her back!"

The insinuation rankled Cole, though he couldn't understand why. "If you say so."

"Damn it man, the whole town knows that," Barrington said with a throaty chuckle. "That one's hotter than a widowed coyote. You know, I hear she likes to be on top. Can't say that I'm surprised. Woman like that..." he rolled his eyes and snorted with disdain, "...wants to be in charge all the time."

Cole didn't like the turn the conversation had taken one bit. He stood up, eager to leave. "If we're through here, I'm going to see how Jesse's faring."

Barrington waved a dismissive hand in the air. "Kid's gonna be just fine."

At the door, Cole muttered, "He damn well better be."

"Before I forget," Barrington said to Cole's back, "the meeting's this Monday. I'll be needing you to join me on this one, all right?"

The tone of Barrington's voice indicated declining

was not an option. Without so much as a backward glance, Cole signaled his approval with a curt nod and slammed the door on his way out.

Chapter 3

The buckboard came to a rumbling halt across the street from the Wells Fargo Bank building. Promptly securing the reins, Cassie scooted to the edge of the wooden, spring seat and leaped to the ground. Juanita, sitting beside her with a white lace-trimmed parasol, dabbed her perspiring temple with an embroidered kerchief.

"*Señorita*," she said, dismounting from the buckboard with dainty steps, "you must not jump down like that! See how they look at you?"

Cassie glanced at the spot on the boardwalk Juanita indicated, seeing the three men gathered a few feet away from the bank. She recognized the whole wretched lot of them. Hired hands at the Triple C. Harmless for the most part with the exception of their leader, Ike Raines, a man she vehemently despised. Not only was the smelly cowpoke Barrington's bootlicker, he went out of his way to harass Cassie any chance he could get.

Like he was doing right now. She glared at him as he blew her a kiss and winked at her.

Raines elbowed the two cowpunchers flanking him, eliciting a fit of laughter from the younger men. She gave all three a poisonous look before turning to address Juanita.

"Just ignore them," she said, walking to the back of the buckboard. She reached for a set of bloated canvas bags, filled with the quarterly earnings to deposit.

"You should have dressed properly," Juanita whispered, grimacing as she eyeballed Cassie's trousers, white cotton shirtwaist, and brown felt duster.

"Nothing wrong with what I'm wearing." Cassie knocked dust from the bags. "Unless you got something more suitable for mucking out the stalls."

"*Si*, but you should have made time to change. You

Dry Moon

must not go around dressed like a man," Juanita said, falling in step behind her.

As they crossed the road, Cassie saw Raines and his two lackeys shift positions. They now stood shoulder-to-shoulder, purposely blocking the bank's entrance.

From behind her, Juanita gasped, stopping in mid-stride. "*Señorita...*" she warned.

"Keep walking Juanita," Cassie ordered, tightening her grip on the moneybags until her knuckles ached.

"Afternoon, Miss Taylor."

Cassie turned her head in time to see Sheriff Logan Brady emerge from his office. Closing the door behind him, the sheriff shouldered his way none-too-gently next to Raines. The latter, visibly flustered by Brady's appearance, stepped onto the sun-parched road. With a whip of his blond head, he ordered his group to follow, and all three men made a beeline for Curly Pete's Saloon.

"Miss Gomez," Sheriff Brady acknowledged, tipping his hat to Juanita, who, smiled in return with unabashed adoration.

"Sheriff," Cassie said, her lungs swelling with relief at his superb sense of timing. She wondered if he'd watched the scene unfold from his office, strategically located next door to the bank.

"Don't pay them no never mind, ma'am. That bunch is always looking for trouble," he said, studying the saloon doors the group disappeared through with iridescent, turquoise eyes. "I'll help you with those." He gave her a charming smile as he relieved Cassie of her bags.

Cassie opened her mouth to protest. A hard pinch from Juanita effectively silenced her.

"*Gracias*, Sheriff," Juanita gushed, elbowing Cassie out of the way. "They are very heavy for us."

"You know," the sheriff began, leading the way inside the bank, "I'd be mighty obliged to escort you when you have bank business to tend to, Miss Taylor."

"I appreciate the offer, Sheriff, but that won't be necessary," Cassie said with a smile.

The sheriff placed the bags on the scarred, wooden floor. "It won't be any trouble."

They stood in line at the teller window, Juanita brushing shoulders with the young sheriff, her eyes riveted on his handsome face. He removed his hat and raked a hand through a mass of wavy, chestnut hair.

"That's quite all right, Sheriff. I manage just fine." Cassie ignored Juanita's petulant stare.

He regarded her intently, his penetrating gaze turning an inky indigo. "All right, ma'am. But if you ever need anything," he said, his expression one of genuine concern, "and I mean anything, you just let me know, all right?"

"I will," Cassie said more to get him to move on than meaning it.

He gave her a warm, dashing smile. "Good," he said, putting his hat back on. "You have a nice day then."

"*Gracias*, Sheriff," Juanita said, flashing him a bright, toothy grin. "You are very kind."

"Just doing my job, ma'am."

"Ahhh." Juanita sighed the moment the sheriff departed. "He is so very handsome, no?"

"Sheriff Brady?" Cassie said aghast.

Juanita nodded with another whimsical sigh, her cheeks blooming with color.

Cassie grunted her disapproval, despite the fact she secretly agreed with Juanita. Tall and broad shouldered, with smoldering good looks, Sheriff Brady was the object of brazen female worship in town. Cassie, however, refused to cater to his physical allure. She thought he was too aware of his good looks for her liking, and besides, he couldn't compare to the perfectly sculpted face consuming her thoughts for days now.

"*Señorita*...you are next." Juanita prodded her with an elbow."

Cassie blinked to attention, noticing the clerk drumming his fingers on the teller window's wooden platform. She smiled apologetically. "Oh, of course."

Once her business in the bank was complete, Cassie headed home. She had plenty of work to finish before sundown, and Juanita needed to get a start on supper. Raul and the men had nothing short of colossal appetites.

"Thank goodness for Sheriff Brady, no?" Juanita said, gripping her seat for support when Cassie steered the buckboard through a particularly rocky trail. "He did not let those men hurt us."

"Raines is the worst of the bunch." Cassie pursed her lips in anger. "He's like a rabid dog. If you show him you're scared, he'll pounce all over you."

"*Si*," Juanita agreed. "You must stay away from him."

"I make it a point to stay far away from Barrington and all his lick fingers," Cassie said, slapping the reins to quicken their pace. "Though I've been wondering how Jesse's faring. I feel horrible about what happened."

"That poor boy," Juanita added softly.

"Damn Raul," Cassie cursed. "I should've had him horsewhipped."

"It would make no difference," Juanita said with a knowing look. "Raul is a very proud man, and he does not like taking orders from a woman. I do not know any man that does."

Cassie nodded in agreement. Raul had become increasingly more difficult since Pa had left her in charge. "Well he's gonna have to get use to taking orders from me," she grumbled. "I already warned him, he gives me any more trouble and I'll let him go."

"Raul worked for your papa for many years, *señorita*. He was always loyal to Don Garrett," Juanita said. "Perhaps he needs more time to adjust."

Cassie gawked at her friend. "More time? We buried Pa seven months ago, and if anything, Raul's gotten worse, not better."

Juanita shook her head. "I worry about you, *señorita*. You have too much responsibility. Perhaps you listen to the sheriff, *si*. Let him escort you to town."

"Sheriff Brady's a busy man, Juanita. I can't rightly expect him to be my personal chaperone, now can I?"

"But the sheriff is the only man who can protect you."

Cassie arched a dark brow. "More like the only man who would bother to. Not like any of the other men in town would be as obliging."

"Bah!" Juanita said with a wave of her hand. "Who cares about them? They gossip about you more than their wives do."

Cassie clenched her jaw, acknowledging that after Barrington, she was the least popular resident in town. Her pa had been well liked among the community. Yet, he too felt the biting sting of wagging tongues because of his unconventional daughter, not to mention the fact her ma had also been her pa's housekeeper, his Mexican housekeeper to boot. Ironically enough, it was the women who spurned her the most. Cassie often overheard them talking disparagingly about her. They scoffed at her manner of dressing, speculated about her mental state, referred to her as 'the crazy breed', knowing she could hear the hurtful things they said. She was never invited to any of their social gatherings, which was fine by her. She didn't want to be around those highfalutin' windbags anyhow.

"And they talk about you because they are jealous," Juanita said, her mocha eyes flaring with heated conviction, "because their fancy husbands look at you with hungry eyes."

Cassie wrinkled her nose. "I don't know about that."

"Well, I do," Juanita said with unyielding certainty. "You do not see it, but you are very beautiful." She smiled then, her gaze softening. "No more of this talk, *si*? I know something that will make you happy."

Cassie gave her a knowing smile. "Really?"

"*Si*," Juanita said with a wink. "Tonight I will make your favorite, chicken mole."

"Want to fatten me up, do you?"

Juanita's eyes brushed the length of Cassie's figure. "You work too hard, and you do not eat enough. You are too skinny."

"I am not," Cassie protested.

"You are."

"I'm not."

"If you say so," Juanita quipped.

"Oh, for goodness sake," Cassie muttered with a roll of her eyes.

"Look," Juanita pinched Cassie's bicep to prove her point, "this is hard from doing man's work. I have to feed you more, so your body will be softer, the way a man likes it, or you will never find a husband."

"Juanita, I'm twenty-nine years old. The way I figure it, marriage passed me by a long ways ago. Besides, the last thing I want is a husband trying to be the boss of me. I like being on my own."

"You talk crazy," Juanita said angrily.

"Do I?" Cassie's voice took on a harder tone. "Then name one man who would be willing to marry me, but still let me run my life as I see fit."

"Sheriff Brady."

Cassie laughed heartily. "I don't know about all that. But it wouldn't work anyhow because you want the sheriff for yourself."

"That is not true," Juanita said, folding her arms across her chest in a show of consternation.

"Uh-huh, that's why you swoon at the sight of him."

Juanita lifted her chin. "So? Just because a man has not made you *swoon*, like you say, does not mean you will not some day."

Cassie sobered immediately. "You're wrong, Juanita," she said, shoving the overpowering memory of dark eyes and fervent hands hot against her skin, way, way back into the cold corners of her mind. "That'll never happen to me."

Chapter 4

Cole stood at the bunkhouse door. His brows knit together at the sight of Katherine perched on the corner of Jesse's bed.

"He's healing quite well," she said with a pleased smile, focusing her warm, honey gaze on Cole.

He cursed inwardly. *Couldn't she keep herself occupied elsewhere?* Her presence here would only bring them all needless aggravation. The entire outfit knew Barrington was as possessive with his wife as he was about all his property. The hands usually scurried like field mice at the mere sight of her, especially when she made these impromptu visits to Jesse. Which she did far too often for Cole's liking.

Without a doubt, she cared about the kid, though. As Jesse equally cared for her. At first, Cole thought Jesse had a crush on Barrington's pretty, young wife. Hell, whenever the kid saw her, his eyes would light up, and he wouldn't stop smiling for days. But Cole had come to realize he was wrong in his assessment. Jesse cared for Katherine like an older sister, while Katherine expressed a genuine maternal concern for the boy, even teaching him how to read and write on his spare time. As for Cole, well, he employed the preferred tactic among all the hands and made himself scarce whenever she was around. Especially when he felt her watching his every move, the way she was doing right now as he approached the bed.

Keeping his eyes purposely trained on Jesse he asked, "Ribs still ache you, kid?"

"A little," Jesse replied, scrunching his freckled nose.

"But he's much better now," Katherine announced. "Rosa is truly gifted. He doesn't have any scars." She smoothed a hand through Jesse's blond curls, sighing with contentment. "Don't you have something to tell Mr. Mitchell, Jesse?"

A blush slowly crept up Jesse's neck, pooling into his freckled cheeks. "It's about Miss Taylor," he began, meeting Cole's direct stare. "She didn't do nothing." He paused to take a breath. "She kept askin' me what I was doing there, but I wouldn't tell her. Reckon she figured I wasn't gonna talk neither, so she let me go. She had them Vargas brothers see me out."

"Damn it, Jess," Cole cursed, giving Katherine an apologetic look for his choice language.

Jesse continued undeterred. "But Villanueva was waiting for me at the gates. He grabbed me and told me he'd shoot me if I hollered. Paco and Mario..." he shook his head as if trying to dispel the memory," ...they didn't do anything, either. They kept arguing with Villanueva in Spanish. I couldn't understand them, but I reckon they were trying to get him to stop."

"Raul Villanueva's always been mean to the bone," Katherine cut in, a scowl marring her delicate features.

Cole swallowed hard. He should've shot that son of a bitch. "Why didn't you tell me sooner?"

"If you'd taken the time to ask, he probably would have," Katherine said.

He cut a sharp glance in her direction. "Pardon me, but some of us actually have to work."

Katherine gave him a cool smile in return. "Strange, here I thought you ran this outfit."

"Hardly," Cole said.

She shrugged and covered Jesse's hand with her own. "Well," she said, rising from her seat. "I must be going, but I'll stop by again tomorrow, all right?"

Jesse's grin stretched from ear to ear. "All right."

At the door, Katherine glanced at Cole over her shoulder. "Mr. Mitchell, a word please?"

Lifting a brow in silent question, Cole followed her outside. He surveyed their surroundings to make sure they were alone.

Katherine's golden gaze also darted about. "I want to ask a favor of you."

Cole paused to study her grim face. "Go on."

"Please watch over Jesse," she said. "He's young and easily influenced by my husband. But he also admires you greatly, and he'll listen to you. I know if you ask him to, he'll stay out of trouble."

Cole was about to reply when movement from the side of the bunkhouse caught his attention. He shook his head in silent warning.

Katherine tensed, her eyes widened with alarm. Without sparing a parting glance at Cole, she ran to the main house.

"Gettin' mighty cozy with the boss's lady." Raines' lanky frame slid along the side of the bunkhouse like a living shadow. "Ain't that right, pretty boy?"

Cole, unperturbed by the accusation, shrugged with indifference. "Know what I think, Raines?"

"What?"

Cole took his time approaching the smug-faced man, stopping when the smell of benzene stung his nostrils. "I think you have to squat to piss," he remarked matter-of-factly.

Raines looked at him with putrefying scorn, fingers curling over his gun holster. "Just 'cos you the boss's favorite now, don't mean it's gonna stay like that forever."

"You fixin' on doing something about it?" Cole challenged, maintaining a deceptively lax posture.

Maybe he could finally get rid of the son of a bitch. Raines had been packing a grudge against him since day one. And the fact that Barrington gave Cole equal say over the running of the outfit as Raines, only made the veteran range boss as sullen as a sore-headed dog.

Raines dropped his hand. "Nah, ya ain't worth the bullet." He spat on the ground by Cole's boot before walking away.

That one's got nothing under his hat but hair, Cole mused, taking his time lighting a cheroot. The man was more a nuisance than a threat. Raines was the kind of man who wouldn't think twice about shooting another in the back. Those were the ones Cole watched out for the most. The cowards.

Cole walked toward the courtyard. He took a seat at the tower fountain, which no longer worked due to the drought. Exhaling a thin plume of smoke, his thoughts leapt yet again to Cassie Taylor. *Damn her fool hide.* She'd let Jesse go, yet she'd carried on as if she were in charge of that whole mess. She would've saved herself a heap of trouble had he known. At that moment, he regretted his actions. He'd been too rough with her. For all her bravado, she was still just a woman. Not like she ever stood a chance against him. Though she probably thought otherwise, he reflected, a smile inching along his face. He closed his eyes, savoring the memory of the way she faced him down, shoulders thrust back like she were royalty, no shred of fear in the depths of those fiery green eyes. He liked that. He liked it too damn much.

****

There were few things in life that compared to the splendor of a long, hot bath. Cassie sighed with pleasure, resting her head against the edge of the wooden tub. Scooting downward, she bent her legs, so only her shoulders and the top of her knees remained exposed. Through the open balcony door of her bedroom, a lazy late-afternoon breeze sent bubbles skimming across the surface of the water. Juanita always got the water just right. Not too hot, not too cold. But the ideal amount of heat to soothe the kinks from her muscles after a long, arduous day.

Reaching for the washcloth, Cassie immersed it in the lavender-scented bathwater and began scrubbing her upper arms with long, lazy strokes. She rubbed her shoulders, stopping to sweep feather-like fingers against her neck. She let her hand rest there, against the rhythmic thumping of her pulse, recalling the moment he held her against the solid, granite mass of his body. His scent, a heady mix of leather, earth, and something uniquely, primitively male assaulted her, and she could swear he was in the room with her. A dull, throbbing heat sprouted at the very core of her, spread along her lower belly. She placed a hand against it, her breath coming in shallow gasps. What was this alien, yet delicious ache that gripped her whenever she thought of Cole Mitchell? And why did she have such little control over it?

Gritting her teeth, she sat up, hugging her knees to her chest. *This was ridiculous.* Two weeks had passed, yet the memory of that blasted man was as crisp as charred paper in her mind. Suddenly angry, she stepped out of the tub and wrapped a towel around herself. Pacing, her feet making wet, slapping sounds on the floor, she cursed Cole

Mitchell. Cursed her absurd fixation on him. A knock at the bedroom door halted her frantic stride.

"*Señorita?*" Juanita called softly.

Grateful for the distraction, Cassie opened the door. "Yes, Juanita?"

"Raul is waiting for you in the kitchen." A troubled expression widened Juanita's dark eyes.

"Has something happened?"

"He would not say, but he is very upset."

"Oh, for goodness sake," Cassie said, twirling on her heel, "tell him I'm coming."

"*Si,*" Juanita said, closing the door softly behind her.

Dressed in denim pants, cotton shirtwaist, and work boots, Cassie hurried to the kitchen, hair still dripping from her bath.

"I am sorry for disturbing you." Raul pressed his hat against his heart in an apologetic gesture.

"What's wrong, Raul?"

Donning his hat again, Raul opened the kitchen door. "Best if you follow me, *si*? I show you."

Cassie followed Raul to the bunkhouse, keeping his brisk pace with little effort.

"See." He pointed to the bunkhouse, where a calf's severed head, pinned with a hunting knife, streaked the white door a bright red.

With mechanical movements, Cassie approached it, swatting the buzzing flies with an absent wave of her hand. "One of ours?" she asked over her shoulder.

"No, *patrona*. I already checked to make sure."

"I was just out here a while ago," she said, her eyes sweeping the vacant surroundings. "Where're the others?"

"It is Friday, remember?" he said, taking a moment to clear his throat. "The men always go to town after they get paid."

"That's right," she said with a caustic grin, "to whore their hard-earned wages away at Curly Pete's."

He had the decency to blush. "*Si.*"

"And you didn't see or hear anything at all?"

"I was not here. I went to the general store for supplies. When I return, I see this." He glanced at the door.

Cassie placed both hands on her hips and looked at

the severed head, scrunching her face with disgust. "Ugh, that poor animal."

"Do not worry, *patrona*, I will see to it that this never happens again."

The heated conviction in his voice troubled her. "No," Cassie said. "I'll fetch Sheriff Brady a-"

Raul interrupted her with a rumbling laugh, staring at her as if she were an obtuse child. "*Chinga la madre*, but you are still so innocent," he said. "You cannot trust the sheriff. He is in Barrington's pocket."

Cassie frowned. "I don't know about that. Brady's always been decent to me and mighty obliging to help in any way."

A wicked grin cracked along Raul's face, his black eyes slid over her figure. "But of course he is. He likes to look at you in your tight pants and your tight shirts."

Cassie's face burned hotter than a flaming stump. "That's enough, Raul."

"Forgive me, *patrona*," he said, turning his face away. "But we both know this is more of Barrington's doing."

"I know that." Cassie gave him a stern look. "I'm warning you Raul, let me handle this. Don't go riding over to the Triple C kicking up a row, do you understand?"

Raul smirked. "You think you are so smart, *eh chiquita*? You think I work with Don Garrett for nothing? It was me," he said, jamming a finger at his own chest, "only me who stood up to Barrington year after year. Me who helped Don Garrett build that canal. Your *pápa*? He stayed in his office, counting the money. His hands, they were so very soft, like a woman's," he said, reaching for Cassie's curled fists.

She was quick to jerk out of his grasp. "I can't believe you would say something like that. You know Pa was too sick to work like he used to."

"But of course, *patrona*." His cryptic smile unnerved her, and she was suddenly eager to get away from him. Turning to leave, she met his even stare over her shoulder.

"Clean this mess up," she ordered, unable to read his shuttered eyes. Not really sure she wanted to.

Chapter 5

Sitting at the wooden desk on the raised platform, Cassie's throat constricted as if cinched tight by an invisible noose. She was not looking forward to today's meeting. Most of the members would undoubtedly object to rationing, but she simply had no other option at this point. She waited as the members filed into the one-room schoolhouse. They took their seats along the wooden benches flanking either side of the center aisle. When she assumed control of Taylor Irrigation and held her first meeting, she realized there was an unwritten rule with regard to assigned seating. To her right, the first bench was reserved for Amos Barrington. To her left, the same was reserved for Cyrus Miller. The proceeding benches were occupied by the remaining members, in seniority and stock-holding order, respectively.

Miller sat in his designated row, accompanied by his range boss, Jake Tanner. Cassie liked Cyrus Miller. Despite the fact that he and Barrington were engaged in a bitter range war, the robust, redheaded Irishman had always been kind to her. He seldom complained, always paid his dues on time, and above all, he was courteous and respectful. He lifted his soft brown gaze to her, nodding a silent greeting. Cassie returned the smile. Though the sight of Jake Tanner in attendance for the second time did not bode well with her.

It was Miller's right to bring anyone he pleased, more so if that person was his range boss. However, Tanner was more than just a range boss. The former slave had a quick draw, made all the more lethal when coupled with his uncanny accuracy. He was a strapping, imposing bear of a man, with glossy, mahogany skin, and matching eyes that seemed to bore right through a person with their intensity. At the previous month's meeting, Barrington accused Miller of rustling some of his longhorns. When

Tanner rose to his boss's defense, Barrington insulted the man with a series of racially charged sobriquets. Tanner's response was a massive, solid fist to Barrington's jaw that sent the rotund cattle baron sprawling on his back, and it took all twelve members considerable effort just to keep Tanner from pummeling Barrington senseless.

"How much longer we gotta wait, Miss Taylor?"

The question came from Nat Olsen, the newest member, sitting in the back of the room.

"We'll start soon as everyone's arrived," Cassie replied, her eyes shifting anxiously to the vacant right front row.

It was as if Barrington purposely sought to aggravate everyone by being consistently late. Cassie took a deep breath, her lungs struggling to expand within the rigid confines of her corset. Though she preferred the liberating comfort of her trousers and linen shirts, she also realized the importance of dressing appropriately when it came to business matters. Today she wore a dark green polonaise dress, a shell cameo brooch adorning its high, lace-trimmed collar. Juanita had taken considerable time arranging Cassie's hair into a loose chignon at the nape of her neck. Unfortunately, some unruly locks, ever with a mind of their own, managed to spring free, particularly at the sides of her face. She looped one such curl behind her ear. From outside, she heard a team of horses and saw Barrington's ornate, fringe-top surrey stop in front of the open schoolhouse door.

"'Bout time," Cyrus grunted.

Cassie almost parroted the sentiment, glaring at Barrington as the portly man ambled inside to his designated bench, with a smug Raines at his side. The sight of Cole Mitchell sauntering into the room moments later robbed her of any ability to speak.

In stunned silence, she could only gape at the gunslinger as he took a seat beside Barrington. As if he felt her eyes on him, he glanced up suddenly, his dark, amused gaze capturing hers. Cassie quickly looked away, cursing the fact he caught her staring.

"Sorry I'm late, folks," Barrington said with a chuckle. He removed his hat and dabbed his balding head with a silk kerchief. "Had me some business to attend."

29

Cassie couldn't seem to keep her eyes from straying to Cole Mitchell. The gunslinger lounged in his seat, one booted foot over the opposite knee, both elbows resting on the back of the bench. He hadn't even bothered to remove his hat, she noted with festering irritation. Instead, he stared at her from beneath the brim, his eyes roaming her face, her shoulders, finally settling on her breasts.

"Amos, kindly tell your guest to remove his hat," Cassie said, tearing her eyes away to stare at the papers on her desk.

"Guest?" Nat Olsen snorted from the back, eyeing Cole scornfully. "That there's a cold-blooded killer."

The sentiment was followed by a series of murmured agreements and expletives. Cassie looked at Cole, realizing none of it was having any effect on the man. If anything, he seemed to relish the negative attention, his mouth curved with a lazy grin, his eyes fastened on hers.

"What you bring the likes of him here for, anyhow?" Olsen directed the question at Barrington. "This ain't no boomtown! This is a quiet, ranching community with decent, God-fearing folks." The young rancher looked at Cassie, his blue gaze beseeching. "Don't mean no disrespect, Miss Taylor, but you should ask the gunfighter to leave. That varmint's got no business here."

"This here's my right-hand man," Barrington interjected. Cassie noticed Raines' surreptitious grin morphing into a scowl with every word. "He goes where I go."

"Thought you already had yourself a range boss," Cyrus remarked.

"Gentlemen," Cassie said, clapping her hands to draw their attention. "Let's move on with the meeting, shall we?"

"My wife refuses to go to town alone, ever since the likes of him showed up." Nat indicated Cole with a thrust of his chin. "There's no tellin' what a man like that is capable of doing to a defenseless woman."

"I've seen your wife, mister," Cole drawled, keeping his eyes on Cassie, "she should be so lucky."

Barrington bellowed with laughter and elbowed Raines who responded with a tight, visibly forced grin.

Nat Olsen jumped to his feet, his fists balled at his

side. "You ain't fit to shine my wife's shoes, you dirty chiseler!"

Cassie sought to maintain some order. "Gentlemen...please..."

"Where's your sense of humor, Nat?" Barrington said between broken chuckles. "Cole's just teasing. I hired him on account of all this rustling going on." He sobered suddenly, glowering at Cyrus Miller. "I got the right to protect my assets any way I can, since the law ain't fit to do so."

"Every man in this room's got rustlers to deal with, ya big blowhard!" Cyrus bellowed. "You hired that gunfighter just so you can peacock 'round town!"

"You shut yer trap, Miller," Barrington said, stabbing a finger in his adversary's direction. "You're the one scaring folks with that filthy, colored-"

"That's enough!" Cassie pounded a fist on the desktop and the entire room fell silent. "This meeting is to discuss company matters. If any of you have other issues you feel are more important, then by all means, leave!"

She waited as the men settled in their seats, giving her their undivided attention. As drops of sweat trailed along the bumpy valley of her spine, she fastened her eyes on Cole.

"Mr. Mitchell, kindly remove your hat, please."

For one gut-cramping moment, she thought he wouldn't comply. He simply stared at her, his eyes hard, challenging. Then his expression softened, and he took his hat off, revealing a head of lustrous, golden brown hair, the ends brushing his collar. He ploughed a hand through it, smoothed the long layers from his eyes. Her breath quickened, catching in her throat as she ripped her gaze away.

"Much obliged," she managed, though her tongue felt like sandpaper.

Cole remained quiet, but continued to observe her. Cassie felt the oppressive weight of his stare with tremors rippling along the length of her limbs. She couldn't recall a time she felt as nervous. Not even when she held her first meeting and didn't know what to expect from the group of men unaccustomed to discussing business matters with a woman. This was a different kind of nervous, though. She hadn't felt her pulse racing then, or her stomach fluttering as if it suddenly sprouted wings.

"Now," she began, opening her leather journal on the desk, "let's start by discussing this drought."

"Ain't nothin' to discuss," Barrington cut in with a saucy smile. "I need more water. It's as simple as that."

"What makes you so special?" Cyrus countered, the fiery color of his face matching his curly hair. "We're all suffering through this, same as you."

"Pardon me, I tried to get here sooner." Sheriff Brady stepped inside the schoolhouse.

"That quite all right, Sheriff," Cassie replied, surprised by his appearance. She motioned toward an empty seat in the back. "You're always welcome here."

Brady gave her a warm smile, but didn't sit where she indicated. Instead, he marched to the front and sat on Barrington's designated bench, leaving space between himself and Cole, who failed to acknowledge the sheriff's presence.

"Please continue, ma'am," Brady said, removing his hat.

Cassie gave him a conceding nod. "This drought's getting worse with each passing day," she said, making eye contact with every member, trying to assess their initial reaction. "The San Pedro River's frightfully low. And we're not the only town relying on it." She took a deep breath before continuing. "I know times are hard, but we can get through this. Summer monsoons are just a few weeks away, but until then, I have to start rationi-"

"Like hell you are!" Barrington jolted from his seat as if it were upholstered with burning coals.

"Sit down, Amos," Brady ordered.

"We all have livestock to feed and crops to raise, Amos," Cassie said.

With a sideward glance at the sheriff, Barrington reclaimed his seat. "Yeah, but nobody here's got as much as I do," he said to Cassie. "You can't cut back my water supply. Hell, what I got now ain't enough!"

"Believe me, I hate doing this." Cassie crossed her arms over her journal. "If there were any other alternative, I would've taken it by now. Unfortunately, rationing is the only way to guarantee we'll all have enough water until the summer rains come."

"Why should I get the same amount of water as Nat does?" Barrington jerked a pudgy thumb to indicate the young rancher. "I got four times as much land."

"I know that," Cassie said. "I'm going to take your individual needs into consideration. But I do have to cut back on everyone's usage."

Barrington gave her a smile that was part sneer. "Even yours?"

"Even mine," Cassie said.

"Don't see what other choice we got," Miller cut in.

"Did you leave your *cojones* back at the ranch, man?" Barrington swept a corrosive look over his rival. "You wanna let this drip-nose of a gal ruin you, then fine. But I won't stand for it."

"Hobble your lip, Amos." Cassie snapped her spine straight, ready for battle. "There's a limit to my patience, and this drip-nose of a gal can cut you clean off whenever she wants. Try to remember that next time you leave dead animals at my door."

Barrington gaped at her, but said nothing. He cleared his throat and fingered the tie obscured beneath his double chin. Next to him, Ike Raines squirmed in his seat like a hooked worm. Cole, however, demonstrated no visible emotion. He returned her stare, his handsome face expressionless, his eyes shuttered.

"Ma'am?" Brady looked at Cassie with a questioning frown.

With a loud 'hmph', Barrington stood and buttoned his frock coat. "I won't sit here and listen to these ridiculous accusations." He crammed his hat on his balding head. "Just make sure you give me the water I'm paying for. You hear me, girl?"

With that, he turned on his heel and departed. Raines was quick to trail after his boss. But it took a moment for Cole to follow suit. When he did, he took his sweet time about it. He donned his hat and lit a cheroot, impervious to the scathing looks most of the members directed his way when he finally sauntered out the door.

"Ma'am?" the sheriff repeated, drawing Cassie's attention back to him.

"It's nothing, Sheriff." Cassie gave him a reassuring

smile, then addressed the members. "Let's move on, shall we?"

Her knotted stomach relaxed as she continued the meeting. As customary, she opened the floor to discussion, taking meticulous notes in her journal. After the hour was up, she concluded the meeting and thanked the members for their participation.

Sheriff Brady approached her as she gathered her belongings. "The meeting went well."

"As good as can be expected," Cassie said, stuffing the journal in her brown leather satchel.

"I didn't mean to impose," he said in an apologetic tone. "But I heard what happened last time between Jake and Amos. Wanted to make sure it wouldn't happen again."

"You weren't imposing," she answered candidly. "I meant it when I said you're always welcome here."

"Thank you, ma'am." Brady's chest swelled with masculine pride. He tipped his hat, signaling his departure. "You have a fine day."

"You too, Sheriff."

When the schoolhouse finally cleared out, Cassie departed. She rounded the corner of the building toward her buckboard, but the sight of Ike Raines sitting in the back, legs swinging over the edge, brought her to a stop.

"Howdy, there," he said, vaulting to the ground. "Meeting's over, huh?"

Glowering at him, Cassie took cautionary backward steps as he neared, acutely aware of their desolate surroundings.

"Your ma didn't teach you no manners?" he asked, closing in on her. He traced the length of her right arm with his forefinger, the leering grin on his face reminded her of a salivating coyote. "I said howdy."

Cassie jerked away. "I'm in a hurry. Let me be."

Raines laughed and lunged for her, but Cassie was ready. From her skirt pocket, she drew a small derringer and placed the barrel against his forehead. She couldn't help but smile at the look of shock blanching his whiskered face.

"Lady said she was in a hurry, Raines." Cole emerged from around the side of the schoolhouse.

Cassie spun her head at the sound of his voice. Though she hated admitting as much, Cole's presence reassured her. She pocketed her gun when he stood in front of her, his tall form serving as her shield.

"Seems to me like you're the one with no manners," he said, hooking both thumbs from his gun belt.

With a snarl, Raines skimmed a hand over his holster. He stopped cold when Cole drew and cocked his gun in one smooth, fluid movement. Cassie blinked, staring at the weapon in Cole's hand with a mixture of awe and bewilderment. He was so fast, she never saw him reach for it.

"Hell, she ain't worth getting shot over."

Keeping a wary eye on Cole's gun, Raines gathered his horse tethered to a nearby tree. He climbed into the saddle and gave them both a venomous look before galloping away.

Cole didn't lower his weapon until Raines was out of view. Turning to face Cassie, he twirled it expertly around a finger and dropped it in its holster.

"Reckon they're worth what you're charging," Cassie said, meeting his level stare. He was tall enough to warrant her lifting her chin to do so, something she seldom did given her own generous height. It was an oddly comforting feeling, having to look up at a man for once.

Up close, she realized his eyes were an unusual hue, not brown as she first thought, but a light brown with flecks of iridescent gold. They reminded her of the color of watered-down whiskey. His features were hard, yet ruggedly sensual, with a long, straight nose and lips too full for a man. Her eyes traced the curve of that generous mouth, and a spark went off somewhere in her nether regions. She admired the expanse of his shoulders, and his whipcord lean physique outlined by his ready-made brocade shirt. Obviously a man who took great pride in his appearance, she surmised, noting his spit-shine leather boots and black felt duster, flapping around those long, powerful legs...

Good Lord, she shouldn't keep gawking at him like this. She met his gaze only to discover he studied her with equal intensity.

"If you're through ogling me," she blurted, growing extremely self-conscious beneath his scrutiny, "I'll be on my way."

A hawkish lift of his brow sent a ripple of heat lapping against her belly. "Hell, I was only returning the favor."

"Don't be ridiculous," she said.

He took a deep breath, as if she were trying his patience. "You going off all alone?"

Cassie snorted, eyeing him with as much scorn as she could muster. "I've been taking care of myself for years, Mr. Mitchell. I could've handled Raines without any interference from you."

"Anybody ever told you you're about as prody as a locoed steer?" He grinned with mild amusement. "Damn shame too, pretty as you are."

His glib tone only fueled her anger. "I don't much care what you think of me," she said, turning around to hide her burning cheeks. He thought she was pretty. "Now if you'll excuse me."

He grabbed her before she could walk away and turned her around to face him. "Wait," he said, pulling her close, "I wanted to talk to you."

Cassie breathed his familiar scent of earth, leather, and raw masculinity. The combination made her dizzy. She pushed away from him. "Don't think we have anything to discuss."

"I know you let Jesse go," he said softly.

Her gaze dropped to the ground. "Yes, I-I've been thinking about him," she stammered, feeling his eyes on her as she rolled a pebble beneath her boot. "But I ain't welcome at Barrington's, as you must know by now. How's he faring?"

"Good as new."

His voice was low, like a throaty whisper, and for a second, Cassie thought she'd imagined the response until she looked at him. He stepped closer, and her eyes dipped involuntarily to those sinfully full lips.

Clearing her throat, she scrambled onto the buckboard, eager to create some distance between them. Looking down at him from her spring seat, she tossed her shoulders back.

"I'm happy to hear that."

"If I were you, darlin'," Cole said, folding his arms across his chest, "I'd get rid of that range boss. He's one bad egg."

His effrontery galled her. "I ain't your *darlin'*, Mr. Mitchell, so quit referring to me as such. And if I needed professional counsel on running my outfit, you'd be the last person I'd ask."

Cole shrugged. "That's the problem with females. No business sense whatsoever."

"At least my business makes me respectable."

"You don't say?" he said with a contrived frown. "You know, working for a woman ain't the easiest thing a man can do. Yet your employees don't seem to mind much. So I'm just curious, darlin'. What do you do to keep your men so..." he snapped his fingers as if searching for the right words," ...*content*?"

"More's the pity..." Cassie angled her head and eyed the length of him, assessing his physical attributes, "...that you'll never know."

He tossed her a devilish grin. "Care to wager on that?"

Conceited lout.

"Rot in hell, Mr. Mitchell."

Slapping the reins across the horse's rump, Cassie set the buckboard in motion and never looked back.

****

"Ya can't trust him, boss," Raines said.

Barrington reached for the cup of coffee Katherine placed before him. He took a sip and felt his throat close up from the bitter taste. "Damn it, woman!" He spewed the dark liquid all over the desktop. "You know I like my coffee sweet. That there's as sour as lemon juice!"

"I'm very sorry, Amos," Katherine replied. She collected his cup and wiped the watery mess with a trembling hand. "I used the last of the sugar on your apple pie."

"Is *that* what that awful mess was?" Barrington shook his head in disgust. "My damn horse feed tastes better than that. Hell woman, what is wrong with you? Are ya so dumb ya can't even figure out how to cook?"

Katherine stared at the ground, her cheeks twin red

caps. "I planned on going to the general store today. But you got back earlier than I expected from your meeting, and...well..."

Barrington massaged his temples. "Just listening to you gives me a headache. Leave us," he said, waving one hand in the air, "me and Ike got business to discuss."

"Of course," Katherine muttered.

Barrington waited for the library door to close behind his wife before addressing Raines. "What's this you were saying about Mitchell?"

From across the mahogany desk, his foreman glowered at him. "I'm sayin' he ain't worth a barrel of shucks! I don't like the son of a bitch, and I don't trust him."

"How many times we gotta go over this, Ike?" Barrington asked. "Ain't nothin' changed, you're still the range boss here, you know that! But Cole's good for business. Ain't had no more rustling since I hired him on." Barrington leaned back in his chair, smiling with satisfaction. "And I know Cyrus is madder than an old wet hen on account of how I outbid him. Hell, even Brady keeps a comfortable distance from me now."

"Mitchell ain't nothin' more than a drifter with a fast draw. You can't trust that sort. He's got no loyalties."

"His loyalty's for sale, Ike, and I'm the only one who can afford it."

"You sure about that?"

Ike's smug grin gave Barrington pause. "Ya got something to say, then spit it out man."

The smile fell from his range boss's face. "I saw Mitchell after the meeting this morning. He waited for the Taylor gal outside and from the looks of them two, I'd say they've been gettin' acquainted behind your back."

"I don't see how," Barrington said, stroking his chin. "I make sure to keep Mitchell plenty busy and as close to me as possible."

"When it comes to some free fuckin', a man always finds a way," Raines snorted.

"Can't argue with that," Barrington mumbled, pushing his chair back to rise. He turned to gaze out the side window.

"What if he likes humping her so much that he turns

on you?" Raines asked. "You don't think she's already thought of that? She's a sly one."

"Just look at that." Barrington indicated the parched range beyond the window with a jerk of his chin. "Drier than a cork leg out there, and she wants to start rationing. Well, I won't let that bitch ruin me."

"I can fix it so you don't have to worry about her no more, boss," Raines said.

With a roll of his eyes, Barrington turned back to his desk. "This better be good, Ike. It was your idea to butcher that lame calf, and it didn't even scare her none."

Raines smiled broadly, revealing a crooked row of yellow teeth. "Nah, that was just for fun." He slid a cautious glance over his shoulder at the closed door. "But I'm done playing games with that uppity bitch. The way I see it, she ain't ever had a man put her in her place yet. Well, I'm fixin' to change all that."

Barrington laced his hands on his belly. "Spare me the details, Ike. I don't rightly care what you got planned. Just as long as nobody can point the finger at me when it's all done, got that?"

"You can count on me, boss."

"I mean it, Ike," Barrington stressed in a grave voice. "No loose ends."

"No loose ends," Raines repeated with a conspiratorial wink.

"Good." Barrington dismissed Ike with a wave of his hand.

Opening the door, Raines bumped into Katherine, who appeared to have been about to knock. "Pardon me, Mr. Raines," she apologized, her eyes downcast.

"What're ya doing out there?" Barrington asked. Suspicion narrowed his gaze. "Thought I told ya to leave us alone?"

"Ma'am." Raines shouldered Katherine aside as he departed.

Katherine wrung her hands in front of her. "I-I was...I mean...I forgot to ask you what you wanted for dinner."

Barrington came around his desk to glower at his wife. "Is that so?"

She nodded a brisk reply.

His gaze moved from her heaving chest to her tiny wasp-like waist. Yes sir, he made sure to get himself the best-looking wife in the territory. He brought a hand to her cheek. "Now that's mighty thoughtful of ya, sweetheart."

Katherine flinched.

Angered by her response, he snarled, "How many times must I tell you not to deny me, woman?"

"I-I'm not," she said, her golden eyes misting with tears. "It's just my womanly flow an-"

Putting all his strength behind the blow, Barrington backhanded her. A surprised yelp escaped Katherine as she staggered backward and landed on the floor. With a fist in her hair, Barrington forced her to her feet again.

"We'll see about that, sweetheart," he whispered in her ear. Her whimpered pleas only aroused him more. He felt himself grow harder as he swiped an arm across the desktop, dumping its contents to the floor.

"A-amos, please, it's my womanly flow," Katherine pleaded between broken sobs.

"Liar!"

He pushed her facedown on the tabletop, hiked her skirts above her rump. Stuffing two fingers into the opening of her drawers, he ripped them aside and realized she was telling him the truth.

Wrinkling his nose with displeasure, he back away from her. "You're disgusting."

"I tried to tell you," Katherine said, her voice a cracked whisper as she straightened and smoothed her skirts. Her bottom lip was swollen, a faint bruise marred her right cheek.

"Soon as your *flow's* done, you better start fulfilling your wifely duties more often, you understand?" Barrington gave her a poisonous look. "I'm sick of your excuses. Doc said there ain't nuthin' wrong with ya, and I need an heir, woman. You gotta tend to my needs, that's your duty. What else you think I got you around for? You ain't but another expense. You and your blasted family."

Katherine remained quiet, hands laced in front of her in demure deference as tears poured down her cheeks.

Barrington circled her. "Quit yer blubberin'!" he ordered. "Ya make me treat you this way. How the hell am I'm supposed to know when you're bleeding or not? Ya lied to me so many times, I can't keep track. Hell, all ya gotta do is spread your legs, woman. What's so hard about that?"

Mute sobs wracked Katherine's delicate frame. She hiccupped, wiped a hand along her runny nose.

"Bah! Go on, get outta here." Grabbing her elbow, Barrington steered her to the door. "Ya make me sick," he yelled before slamming it shut.

Stupid cow. He should've left her in that shack with the rest of her starving kin. At first, her purchase seemed like a sound investment. He'd procured a young, fertile wife in the cusp of her breeding years. Why, she should be able to give him all the sons he desired for years to come. She was also the best-looking gal around, and a man like him could settle for nothing less. But she was sorely trying his patience. The entire time he lavished her with fine jewelry and expensive gifts, shacked her up in this fine home, paid for her ma's medicines and her sister's schooling. And what did she give him in return? Nothing. Nothing but that cold, remote attitude as if she were, and always had been, too good for him.

He didn't like the fact that she was always hanging around when he discussed business matters, either. Everybody knows women ain't got the mental aptitude for such things. He failed to understand her evident interest. His suspicious nature told him he should keep a closer eye on the little missus.

And that's exactly what he was going to do.

Chapter 6

The first week of June closed with no rain. Though the average daily temperature soared to above sweltering, a welcome harbinger as far as Cassie was concerned. She knew behind the stifling heat came the summer monsoons. With this knowledge, she relished the sweat trickling down the nape of her neck, pasting her linen shirt to her torso as she forked hay into the barn stalls. Taking a moment to relax, she hung the pitchfork on the wall. She reached for the water canteen hanging from the peg beside it and took several thirsty gulps. Her stomach grumbled, reminding her of its vacant state, and she decided to finish the stalls after a mid-morning snack. She almost reached the back door when Paco came running out, crashing into her.

"I am so sorry, *patrona*," he said, one hand holding her arm until Cassie regained her balance.

"Look where you're going!" Juanita reprimanded Paco as she shouldered him aside.

Cassie noticed the grim look on both their faces. "What's wrong?"

It was Paco who spoke first. "*Patrona*, it is Raul. He is in jail."

Cassie's stomach dropped a grim peg. "Jail?" she repeated. *What did Raul get himself into now?* "Thought you two went to the general store for supplies?"

"*Si*." Paco nodded his head. "It is there we ran into Barrington. When Raul saw him, he went loco. He called him a coward and drew his gun. I tell him to put his gun away, *patrona*, I swear it. But he would not listen to me. He almost killed Barrington, but that *pistolero* shot Raul instead."

"Cole Mitchell shot Raul?" Cassie tried to keep her voice calm. *Good Lord this was worst than she anticipated.* "Is he hurt bad?"

"No." Juanita spoke for the young man. "Paco says Sheriff Brady took him to jail and is waiting for you there. You must hurry, *señorita*."

Without dallying a moment longer, Cassie said to Paco, "Saddle my horse."

"*Si, patrona*," he said, dashing toward the stables.

Cassie then looked at Juanita. "I'll need my gun."

With a swift nod, Juanita ran inside the house and returned seconds later with Cassie's gun belt in her right hand and her felt Stetson in the other.

Cassie put both items on. "I won't be long, Juanita."

"Your horse is ready, *patrona*," Paco called as he emerged from the stables, leading the brown mare by the reins. He waited for Cassie to climb into the saddle before handing them to her.

"Please be careful, *señorita*," Juanita said.

Cassie nodded once before galloping away. She rode like a mad woman, cursing Raul the entire time. Hadn't she specifically ordered him to stay clear of Barrington just a couple weeks back? Blast his stubborn hide.

She reached town in record time and spurred her mount to the water trough located in front of the saloon. Dismounting, she slapped trail dust from her shirt and trousers as she walked across the street to the sheriff's office. Once inside, she saw Sheriff Brady sitting at his desk. Barrington sat across from him, accompanied by Cole Mitchell, who leaned against the wall with arms folded across his chest. Cassie looked at the holding cell adjacent to the sheriff's desk, where Raul lay on a small cot. Soft snores escaped through his parted lips. His right arm was draped over his eyes, blocking the sunlight pouring in through the tiny window above him.

Cassie made sure to keep her gaze on Brady when she spoke. "Good morning, Sheriff."

Brady rose to greet her. "Mighty grateful you made it here so fast, ma'am."

"In a hurry to fetch your scalawag, are ya?" Barrington asked.

Cassie ignored the miserable swine. "What happened, Sheriff?"

"Well, ma'am," Brady jerked his head toward the holding cell, "Raul tried to shoot Amos outside the general

43

store."

"That dirty son of a Mexican whore!" Barrington exclaimed. "Tried to shoot me in the back, he did. I wasn't lookin' for no trouble, either." The pig shook his head, evidently relishing his newly acquired victim role. "I told him so, and I got me a whole town of witnesses that'll back me up. I'd a been a goner, if Cole hadn't shown up."

Cassie forced herself not to look at Cole, though she felt him staring at her, and was suddenly painfully aware of her sullied attire.

"Raul's no back shooter," she said.

"Like hell he ain't."

Cassie whipped her head to glower at Cole. Her retort expired on her lips with the rancorous look he gave her.

"He did try to shoot Amos in the back, Miss Taylor. I saw it myself." Brady's voice held a bit of regret.

"What are you going to do with him?" Cassie asked the sheriff, her eyes on Raul.

"That all depends on Amos." Brady looked at the cattle baron.

"Look here, girl," Barrington rose from his seat, "just to show you I can be right neighborly myself, I won't bring no charges against Villanueva." He clapped his beefy hands. "In fact, let's forget about this whole thing. You can let him go, Sheriff."

"You sure about this, Amos?" the sheriff asked with some reserve.

"Of course," Barrington insisted. He donned his hat and motioned for Cole to follow him. "Why this whole experience has made me realize how lucky I am to be alive! Come on Mitchell, I'm in the mood to celebrate."

Cassie stood fuming as the pair departed, wanting to slap that smug grin off Barrington's face. She knew damn well he wasn't being neighborly. He had something up his sleeve. She could smell it. Now, she was beholden to that insufferable boor.

The sound of Brady's voice pulled her from her angry ruminations. "Mitchell almost shot his hand clean off."

Cassie snapped to attention. "I'm sorry, Sheriff, what did you say?"

Brady strolled to the holding cell, waved a hand for

Cassie to join him. "Look," he said, pointing to Raul.

Peering in between the bars, Cassie noticed Raul's bandaged right hand. "How bad is it?"

"I got the doc to stitch him up," Brady said. "Gave him some laudanum for the pain, that's why he's out." He shook his head with some disbelief. "You know, I've seen a lot in my day, ma'am, but I ain't ever seen a faster draw than Mitchell." Cassie bristled at the admiration in his voice. "He shot the gun from Raul's hand, then put a hole clear through the middle, all with little effort and even less feeling. Doc said the bullet severed all the tendons. Raul won't ever regain full use of that hand."

Cassie shook her head sadly. "Does Raul know that?"

"Not yet. You want to tell him, or you want me to do that?"

Sighing, Cassie turned away and walked to the front window. She stared at the bustling road outside. "I think he'll take it better if it's coming from you. Let him sleep for now."

"All right."

Cassie gave him a rueful look. "Sheriff, I do apologize for-"

"None of that now," he interrupted. "You ain't responsible for Villanueva. He's always had a hankering for trouble. It was just a matter of time before something like this would happen. 'Sides, Barrington's got more enemies than he can keep track of. Raul won't be the last man to try to shoot him in the back."

The scorn in his voice was evident in every word. Cassie contemplated him a moment. "You don't like Amos, do you?"

"My job is to uphold the law, ma'am," Brady said. "Personal feelings got nothing to do with it."

"Of course."

"He could've killed him, you know." Brady's sharp, blue eyes searched her face. "Mitchell doesn't miss."

"So he was being merciful?" she asked with a mirthless grin. "Is that it?"

"Can't rightly say." Brady shrugged. "That man's a puzzle to me."

Clenching her jaw, Cassie opened the door. "I gotta head back, Sheriff. I appreciate your having the doc tend to Raul. That was very kind of you."

Brady gave her his trademark, dashing smile. Cassie thought he would make a mighty fine politician if he ever chose that route. "Just doing my job, ma'am. You have a good day."

"Likewise, Sheriff," she said, closing the door softly behind her.

****

Sitting at a table by the front windows of Curly Pete's Saloon, Cole lit a cheroot as he watched Cassie collect her horse at the water trough. He leaned forward to get a better view of her as she climbed into the saddle, admiring her lusciously rounded bottom, outlined by those tight trousers she wore. He also realized, with mounting irritation, he wasn't the only man appreciating her physical assets. A group of young cowpunchers on the boardwalk watched with bulging eyes as she spurred her mare forward, her breasts bouncing quite indecently when she broke into a full gallop. She sat astride, too, he noted, not particularly surprised by that fact.

Muttering a vile curse, Cole reached for his whiskey and tossed it back, the fiery liquid singed a trail down his throat. She should know better than to come to town dressed like that. Not even them cheap whores upstairs would dare venture outside in a pair of trousers. He took a drag of his cigarette, recalling how stunning Cassie looked in that meeting with her green dress; glossy, raven tresses swept up to reveal a creamy, elegant neck. And those catlike green eyes, peering at him seductively beneath half-mast lids. Hard to believe it was the same woman who walked into the sheriff's office today, strands of hay sticking out of her braid, her face smudged with dirt. Yet, he still found himself savagely drawn to her. Though he felt more like strangling her for ignoring him the entire time and for defending that lily-livered range boss of hers. Just what kind of relationship did she and Villanueva have, anyhow?

"Mitchell!" Barrington shouted, waving an arm to draw Cole's attention from the other side of the room.

Cole refilled his glass and watched Barrington walk toward him with mild irritation. *Poor bastard really thinks I saved his hide.* Truth is, he wouldn't have raised a finger in Barrington's defense had Villanueva faced him like a man. But if there was anything Cole despised, it was a back shooter. Though, the only thing Villanueva's gonna be shooting from now on is the breeze, he thought with a satisfied smirk.

"This here's the good stuff," Barrington announced, slapping a new whiskey bottle on the tabletop in front of Cole. He poked a pudgy thumb at the wooden stairwell beside the bar. "Got me some female company. Care for some? I always get the best in the house, but I told Pete to save her for you today."

Cole eyed the ragtag group of semi-clad women draped over the banister on the top landing, exposing their abundant charms. Why Barrington would rut with the likes of any of them when he had a beautiful wife at home was beyond Cole's understanding. He reached for his drink and raised it toward Barrington in a silent toast. "Much obliged, but I'll pass."

"You'll pass?" Barrington repeated, clearly offended by the refusal. "What's the matter? Saving yourself for the Taylor woman?"

Cole's glass stopped midair. "Who, what, or where I fuck is none of your concern, old man."

"Don't get your dander up." Barrington chuckled. "I was just foolin'." He patted Cole's shoulder sympathetically. "'Sides, I hear you gotta pay twice as much for half the fun with her. Just ask Villanueva!"

He shot Barrington a murderous look as the portly man disappeared up the stairs with surprising speed. Cole grabbed his abandoned drink, draining the contents in one fierce gulp. He shouldn't give a damn who Cassie's been screwing. If anything, he should be grateful she was experienced, it would serve to facilitate his conquest. No wonder she wasn't married yet. What man in his right mind would saddle himself with a woman like that? No, that little hellion was the kind of woman a man took to his bed and none-too-gently either. And it was his bed she'd be in next, of that he was certain. He envisioned her on her back, long, sleek legs parting for him, or on her hands and knees, or on top, riding the hell out of him. He didn't really give a damn which way he had her. But he would have her, and he would have his fill.

Chapter 7

After three days, Raul returned to the ranch. Cassie received him with a wooden smile and a cordial handshake. Though tightlipped about the transpired events, he was uncharacteristically humble and soft-spoken. With his injured hand there was limited work he could do, but Cassie let him settle into the bunkhouse just the same. She'd wait until the end of the workday before handing Raul his final paycheck.

When that time came, she sat at the kitchen table, her fingers drumming against the tabletop as the back door opened.

"Juanita said you wanted to see me?" Raul asked, walking inside.

Cassie maintained a guarded expression as she rose from her seat. She gestured for Raul to take the empty chair opposite her. "Please, sit."

Raul's perceptive, dark gaze shifted to the white envelope lying in the middle of the table. "I prefer to stand, *patrona*."

Cassie steeled her spine. "You leave me no choice, Raul. I told you to stay out of trouble, and let me deal with Barrington. But what did you do? You tried to shoot the man in broad daylight. In the back no less!"

Raul's composure never faltered. "Barrington is a coward. He deserves to die as one."

"You're the one who looked like a coward, don't you see that?" Cassie folded her arms across her chest. "I never thought you would stoop so low as to shoot a man in the back, even if it was Barrington. What's worse, is that I'm beholden to him now. That's the only reason he told the sheriff to let you go."

"You are not beholden to him, *patrona*," Raul said with a scowl. "I will go back to the sheriff and tell him to hang me."

"Don't be ridiculous!"

"It is better than living like this." He raised his injured hand. "I will not use it again."

"I am truly sorry, Raul. But you have only yourself to blame."

He stared at her, his eyes dimming with each word. "Who is going to hire a cripple?"

"You're not a cripple." He would not manipulate her into feeling sorry for him. "You're very skilled, and you'll have no problems finding work elsewhere." Cassie pushed the envelope across the table. "I've paid you for the entire month. There's also a bonus check in there for all your years of service, and a letter of recommendation. You can stay until the end of the week, if you like."

To her surprise, Raul did not argue. Instead, he reached for the envelope, and stuffed it in his front shirt pocket. "That is not necessary. I will leave first thing tomorrow." He nodded once before walking out the door.

Cassie took a deep breath. She just fired the man who built this ranch alongside her father, the only man her father trusted implicitly. How could it have come to this?

"*Señorita*," Juanita said, joining her in the kitchen. "How did it go?"

"Remarkably well," Cassie said with a frown. "I never expected Raul to react so...calmly."

"He is staying until the end of the week, then?"

Cassie shook her head as she reached for the coffee pot on the stove. She poured herself a cup, grimacing when she swallowed the cold, unsweetened liquid. "No, he's decided to leave tomorrow."

Juanita rolled a shoulder. "If that is what he wishes, then all is well."

"Don't know about that. Got a heap of work around here, Juanita," Cassie reminded her. "I need all the help I can get."

"Everything will be fine."

Cassie ran a weary hand through her long hair. "I'll worry about that tomorrow. I'm beat. I'm gonna wash up and turn in." She emptied her cup in the sink and headed toward the door. "Good night."

"*Buenas noches.*"

Cassie strolled down the hall, her boot heels tapping against the red ceramic floor. When she walked by the parlor, movement at the front windows caught her eye. She stopped short, and went to investigate, one hand resting on her gun holster. Behind the wood framed sofa, one of the windows was open, its sheer, lace curtains ruffled softly with an early evening breeze.

Shoving it aside, Cassie poked her head out. Nothing but warm, dry air greeted her from the vacant front porch. She closed the window and snapped the lock in place. Hurrying to her room, she made a mental note to remind Juanita not to leave the windows open at night.

****

Cole saw the shadowy figure creep along the bunkhouse and stop to peer into the window. He recognized the slim form even before her perfume gave her away. She might as well have been wearing a cowbell.

"Ma'am," he said, purposely startling Katherine.

She faced him with eyes bulging and hand over her heart. "Oh my goodness," she exclaimed. "You scared the life out of me."

"Go home, ma'am. You don't want your husband catching you out here."

She shook her head. "I waited until Amos was sleep. I must talk to you, Mr. Mitchell, please," she implored him. "It's dreadfully important."

Despite his better judgment, Cole led her to the bunkhouse. He ensured it was empty before escorting her inside.

Cole leaned a shoulder against the closed door. "What is it?"

"I didn't know what to do." Katherine's voice trembled as she spoke. "I-I overheard a conversation a while back. I didn't think Amos was serious. I thought it was all talk...I..."

Cole placed a firm hand on her arm. "Relax," he said in a soft voice. "Just relax, all right? You're not making any kind of sense."

Katherine stared at the floor, her eyes pooled with unshed tears. "I fear Miss Taylor's in danger. I saw Ike leave earlier with some strange men. They were headed to her spread. They talked about doing some awful things to that poor woman."

An icy hot feeling slithered in Cole's gut. "How long ago?"

"About an hour."

"How many men?"

Katherine blinked, her pretty face puckering with a frown. "Um...there were four, including Ike."

With a curse, Cole reached for his gun belt draped over the bedpost. He strapped it around his hips. "Go home," he said. "I'll handle this."

Katherine followed him to the door and grabbed his arm before he could leave. "Mr. Mitchell?"

He turned to look at her, one brow arching.

"You mustn't tell anyone that I told you," she said. "My ma's very ill, the doctors and medicines...are very expensive. And my sister needs schooling, and she's so young." She wiped a fat tear away. "I know my husband is not a good man, but he's the only person who can help my family. Please give me your word you won't tell anyone."

He regarded her a silent moment. "You have my word."

Chapter 8

A hand on her shoulder shook Cassie awake.

"*Patrona*, wake up!"

Another hard shake. With a groan, Cassie rolled onto her side and opened her eyes. She looked at Raul who stood by her bed, a revolver in his good hand. "Raul?" She sat up with a start. "What's wrong?"

"There is someone in the house. I saw him sneaking in the back door."

"Are you sure?" Her heart pounded. "Where're the others?"

Raul brought a finger to his lips, motioning for her to keep quiet. "Juanita is coming. Paco and Mario are waiting for me in the hall. You stay here with Juanita. Lock the door, and do not let anyone inside, *si*?"

He was gone before Cassie could voice her disapproval. Almost immediately, Juanita darted into the room and climbed onto her bed.

"*Madre de Dios*," Juanita's voice was a scratchy whisper, "what are we going to do?"

Cassie bolted out of bed. "You're going to stay here while I help Raul and the boys."

"No. Raul said it is safer if we stay here."

"This is no time to argue," Cassie said, opening her dresser. She pulled out a pair of black trousers and a linen shirtwaist.

Dressing with haste, she handed Juanita the derringer she kept inside her jewelry box and then reached for her own revolver, snapping the chamber open to ensure it was loaded.

"Don't worry," she said, patting Juanita's hand. "We'll be all right. Just lock the door behind me."

"Be careful." Juanita's eyes watered.

Cassie managed a tight smile and ventured into the darkened corridor. From the kitchen came a scuffling sound, and cocking her gun she headed in that direction when a gunshot rang out. Cassie stopped mid-stride, choked on the acrid scent of gunpowder, her heart thundering in her chest. Summoning all her courage, she shouldered the swinging door open and discovered Raul face up on the kitchen floor. She looked over his lifeless body, a lump of bile catching in the back of her throat. His mouth hung open, his black vacant stare fixated on the ceiling. Beneath him, a puddle of blood glittered like tar in the moonlight.

Cassie clamped a hand over her mouth to keep from screaming. Hot tears welled up in her eyes, but she blinked them back. The last thing she needed was to fall apart at a time like this. She needed her wits about her. Keeping her eyes averted, she stepped over Raul's body and slipped through the back door.

Outside, her eyes probed the inky night, but couldn't discern any visible shapes in the looming darkness. She'd barely placed one foot in front of the other when someone grabbed her from behind. A gloved hand curled around her wrist and squeezed. Cassie tried to break free to no avail. Her palm throbbed with a dull pain, her fingers went limp, and she dropped her gun.

Steel arms wrapped around her midsection, lifting her off her feet. With a curse, Cassie pushed against her assailant, kicking the black, empty air in a futile attempt to throw him off balance. Another arm coiled and tightened around her throat, cutting off her air supply. She struggled for breath, her vision swirling like a funhouse bull's-eye as her assailant dragged her into the barn. Once inside, Cassie rammed an elbow into her captor's midsection with all her might. She heard a grunt and suddenly she was free. She ran, the adrenaline surging through her body granting her uncanny speed. Her fingertips almost touched the barn doors when an arm swung from the darkness, and a fist connected with her jaw.

Cassie reeled to the ground. The warm, coppery rush of blood filled her mouth. She brought a finger to her lips, ensuring her teeth were all intact. This time she heard laughter-deep, husky, masculine laughter-as a hand ploughed through her hair, snapping her head back. She

53

cried out with the biting pain of her scalp and came face-to-face with Ike Raines.

"I knew you was a strong one." He chuckled and shoved her forward. "That's why I brought me a friend."

Cassie turned her head to see another man emerge from the shadows. The burly, dark-haired stranger raked the blade of a large hunting knife across the stubble on his chin. He looked down at her with a grin that chilled her bones.

"She put up quite a fight outside, huh?" the knife wielder asked Raines.

"Yeah," Ike said. He smiled with predatory glee as he removed one glove, then the other, stuffing them both in his back pocket. "I like me a woman with some fire."

Cassie stared at both men. Her stomach writhed with a sick feeling. Panic settled over her like an icy cape. Without a second thought, she bolted. She managed to get as far as the second stall, when someone tackled her from behind.

With a massive hand on her ankle, the dark-haired one dragged her beneath him. He laughed as he wrestled with her, pinning her wrists above her head with one hand. He brought his hunting knife against her throat with the other. Cassie stilled beneath the sharp blade pricking her larynx.

"I get her first," Raines order.

Cassie watched Raines undo his pants with maddening haste, as his partner shifted to kneel opposite her head, allowing Raines access to her body. Ike squatted before her, and she lashed out, kicking him in the stomach.

"Bitch!" he squawked, grabbing her ankles and pulling them apart.

He knelt between her spread legs, striking her across the temple with his gun. Cassie's head exploded with pain, her vision blurred as rough hands ripped her chemise, cold fingers dug into the tender skin of her exposed breasts.

"Get off me!" she screamed.

But all she heard was their commingling laughter. Bile clumped in the back of her throat like packed earth while she fought back tears, refusing to accept the inevitable. Like a wild horse, she bucked and wriggled beneath Raines, turning her face when he tried to kiss her. He grabbed her chin in a bruising grip, crushed his mouth over hers. Cassie choked on his foul breath, her stomach heaved when he thrust his tongue into her mouth. She bit down with all her strength. With a yelp, Raines jerked his head away. He wiped blood trickling from one corner of his mouth with the back of his sleeve.

"You're going to pay for that you whore!"

He pistol-whipped her a second time. A burning pain, like a surging geyser, filled Cassie's head. Her body went limp, and she closed her eyes, only fractionally cognizant of Raines fumbling with her trousers, pulling them over her hips. A gunshot rang out then, loud enough to puncture the thunderous pounding in her ears. It took a moment for Cassie to realize her hands were free.

Opening her eyes, she focused her grainy vision on Ike's face as it contorted with mute horror. She followed his line of vision and saw his accomplice hunched over; blood trickled from a hole in his temple.

"Get up."

Recognizing the voice, Cassie began to sob. From fear or relief, she wasn't sure, and didn't really care.

Raines stumbled to his feet. "Take it easy, Mitchell. I wasn't gonna hurt her."

"You got that right," Cole said in a menacing whisper.

Cassie rolled onto her side, clutched her shirtwaist closed with a fisted hand. She tried to stand, but her limbs felt like wet noodles. The pain in her head intensified, roared in her ears. Through her watery vision, she saw Cole holster his weapon and flex his fists. Raines backed away from him, fastening his trousers with trembling hands.

"She was hot for it, Mitchell," he said. "Hell, this was our second go-round. She plumb attacked me when I told her I wouldn't turn on Amos. I was just defending myself."

Rage allotted her a moment of strength. In a dry, hoarse voice Cassie yelled, "Liar!"

Her outcry failed to draw Cole's attention. He was too focused on Raines, stalking the man like a predatory feline. Raines did look her way and tripped over a haystack as a result. Before he could rise, Cole delivered a swift kick to his stomach.

"Stop! I ain't done nothin' to her," Raines squealed.

Cole kicked him a second time, his boot landed against Ike's ribs with a sickening thud that made Cassie cringe.

"I said get up." Cole's voice left no doubt to his intent.

Raines made a small, guttural sound, but regained his footing. Pulling a knife from his back pocket, he slashed at Cole who ducked and swerved to avoid the blade. Raines became reckless, slashing at the empty air in wide, sweeping arches.

A gust of smoke smothered Cassie's scream. She coughed, looked all around. *Fire!* The barn was on fire. Flames licked the walls, dripped like liquid from the ceiling, igniting whatever it landed on. Around her, smoke thickened, coalesced into a black cloud that stung her eyes and clogged her throat. Cassie struggled for breath, her lungs felt as if they burned from the inside. Desperate for air, she crawled toward the barn door. It seemed so far away. So out of reach. She'd never make it.

Her breathing became a labored, high-pitched wheeze as smoke filled her lungs. Like a broken rope, consciousness slipped from Cassie's fingers, until she finally collapsed.

Chapter 9

Cassie's eyelids fluttered open. It took a moment for her eyes to adjust to the harsh, morning light. Blinking, she was able to make out the image of Juanita staring at her with wide, wet eyes.

"*Madre Santa!*" she cried, throwing both arms around Cassie.

"Juanita, you're strangling me."

"Oh, forgive me." Juanita released her. "I am just so happy you are alive."

Cassie sat up, wincing when her head began pounding with the force of a sledgehammer. She touched the source of the pain, felt a bandage around her head. Ignoring Juanita's protests, she removed it, her fingers trailing along a sticky gash above her left temple. Pulling her hand away, Cassie stared at the brownish, crusty blood on her fingertips.

"I wrapped it for you," Juanita said. "I stopped the bleeding."

"What happened?" Cassie asked.

Juanita gave her a horrified look. "You do not remember?"

Cassie inhaled. Her aching lungs brought the images back, merged her piecemeal thoughts with gruesome clarity. She recalled Raul's lifeless body in the kitchen, how Raines and that stranger tried to rape her in the barn. Had it not been for Cole...

"Cole!" she gasped.

Had he made it out of the barn?

"He is fine, *señorita*," Juanita assured her.

"Thank goodness," Cassie expelled in a breath.

She grabbed the duster she wore with tremulous fingers, and noticed it for the first time. It was much too big, and wrapped around the entire length of her body. She unbuttoned it, glimpsed the frayed remains of her shirtwaist and chemise beneath.

"It is *señor* Mitchell's coat," Juanita said. "He took you out of the barn. He tells me Ike Raines is dead, *señorita*."

Cassie swallowed around the acrid lump in her throat. "Cole saved my life."

Juanita nodded slowly. "*Si*."

"My God." Cassie looked at the charred remains of her ranch. There wasn't a single structure left standing, even the privy hadn't been spared. She closed her eyes, fighting back tears as Juanita detailed the events.

"Those men were going to kill us!" she said. "They set the house on fire. Thank *la virgencita* for *señor* Mitchell! He killed those bad men! And he helped me escape. But the others..." she paused to swallow through her tears, "...they did not make it."

Cassie choked on her own salty tears. "Are we the only ones left?"

Juanita nodded. "But the *señor* is coming for us. He went to get some supplies, so I stay here watching you. He is going to take us to a safe place."

"What safe place?" Cassie asked.

Juanita did not respond. She appeared preoccupied, her narrowed gaze riveted on the horizon. Then a smile brightened her face, and she jumped to her feet, shielding her eyes from the encroaching sun.

"What are you looking at?" Cassie asked, unable to see anything from her vantage point.

"He has returned!" Juanita cried.

Recognizing Cole's horse in the distance, Cassie curled her fists, wishing the ground would drop open and swallow her whole. Had he believed Raines' filthy lies? *She was so humiliated.* She hadn't done anything wrong. But Cole had seen her under such dehumanizing circumstances. It was more than she could bear. Cassie munched on her bottom lip, wincing in sudden pain. She'd forgotten about that injury. *I'm such a mess.*

She watched Cole approach her with Juanita trailing behind. Cassie stood up, her chest heaved from the effort. Beneath her watery legs, the ground spun like a toy top. She closed her eyes and staggered forward, landing against a metal plate of a chest. Strong arms wrapped around her, held her upright. It was a moment before she could lift her head to stare into that whiskey gaze.

"Have you no common sense, woman," Cole said.

"Are you okay, *señorita*?" Juanita asked, rushing to Cassie's side.

Cassie moved away from Cole. "I'm fine."

With tiny backward steps, she put as much distance between them as she could. Juanita shadowed her, lending a supporting arm in the process.

"You feel well enough to ride?" Cole asked, his eyes searching her face.

Cassie nodded, and released Juanita's hand to demonstrate she could stand on her own. "Where we going?"

"The hell away from here," he said, grabbing the crook of her elbow.

"But I have to see the sheriff!" Cassie wriggled her arm free.

Cole rounded on her. "What for?"

"What for?" Cassie shook her head and looked all around. "This is Barrington's doing, and I want him strung up by his fat neck!"

"Based on what?" Cole stared at her. "It's your word against his."

"This is true, *señorita*," Juanita pointed out.

Cassie shot Juanita a warning look, and then turned her incensed gaze on Cole. "Ike's body is in there!" She pointed to the smoking rubble behind her.

"That doesn't mean squat. Raines could've acted alone. Barrington will sure as hell say that he did. The whole town knows Ike had a mean hankering for you. 'Sides, his wife, plus a ranch full of men will say Barrington never left the hacienda last night."

"That includes you?" she asked, looking him square in the eye.

His handsome face closed up. "He was home all night. That's a fact."

"That doesn't mean he didn't send Ike and those men." Cole returned her level stare, his continued silence prompting her to add, "But you already know that, don't you?"

"Listen, I'm real sorry about all this," his expression

softened, "but you're in no shape to fend for yourself, much less make any sensible decisions. If you don't care for your own well-being, then do it for Juanita." He turned to his mount. "I'm headed for Shillings. You wanna wire the sheriff, or send a lynch mob for Barrington after that, you go right ahead."

Cassie marveled at the smooth way he shirked her questions. She was both too physically and emotionally exhausted to press him further, at least for the time being. And he *did* make a solid argument about Juanita. "What's in Shillings?"

"My sister runs a boarding house there," he said over his shoulder. "You ladies can stay with her as long as you need."

Cassie chewed the delicate skin around her fingernails. A nervous habit she thought she'd broken years ago. "You have a sister?"

She hadn't intended to voice the thought.

Cole kneed his horse toward her. "Yep. Reckon I'm human after all."

"*Señorita,*" Juanita took her hand, "we go with him, *si?*"

"You don't have to come, Juanita," Cassie acknowledged with a heavy heart. "You got your kin. You'll be safer with them."

Juanita's dark eyes glimmered with unshed tears. "I am with my kin. And now we must go."

"Listen to the gal," Cole told Cassie.

Cassie ran a critical eye over his copper stallion. "Don't think there's room for three of us on there."

"That's why I fetched us some spares." He gestured behind her with his chin.

Cassie spun her head, her eyes scanning the ridge. She saw a golden palomino, and a spotted appaloosa, both animals chomping happily on some sparse shrubbery.

"*Diosito!*" Juanita raced to inspect the appaloosa, making her choice obvious. She ran a hand over the leather saddle. "He is beautiful. You are very kind, *señor.*"

"Get a wiggle on," Cole said, shielding his eyes beneath his hat. "We ain't got all day."

Cassie strode to the palomino, her throat compressing with emotion as she stroked its muscular flank. Climbing into the saddle, she took firm hold of the reins. She brought her mount in line behind Cole, following his lead as he rode north. Juanita galloped past her, apparently eager to ride alongside Cole.

Cassie watched them riding ahead, unaware the gap between them grew larger as she lagged behind. She let the palomino control the pace as she shifted in the saddle. She ached all over, and couldn't seem to find a comfortable position that didn't make some sore spot scream in protest. Her head throbbed with a sharp, pulsating pain. She rubbed her eyes with the heel of her palm.

Up ahead, Juanita stopped short, turning around to stare at Cassie. She shouted something to Cole, who also turned his mount. Cassie couldn't make out the words. Funny that everything seemed to be growing darker around her. She watched Juanita and Cole ride toward her, and fast. What were they doing? Didn't they know she would catch up?

The dark fog crowding her vision suddenly blinded her, and the next thing she felt was the ground break her fall.

****

Cassie heard her name called, but couldn't respond. She was so tired. She wanted to remain in the dark, soothing abyss where she hovered weightless as a tree leaf. The insistent voices bled into her dream, like spectral fingers prying her eyes open. She blinked and looked all around, momentarily disoriented. Someone cradled her, and she tilted her head, meeting Cole's stormy gaze.

"What happened?"

"You fell off your horse," he answered, his dark gaze studying her.

Embarrassment consumed her. *Falling off her horse like some greenhorn!* The last thing she remembered was the throbbing pain in her head.

"Oh, I must've dozed off," she lied, trying to make light of the events. "I'm fine now, really."

"I don't think so," Cole said. "You're likely to break your neck next time."

"Don't be silly. I learned how to ride before I learned

how to walk," she persisted, sitting upright.

"Just the same, you should ride with Juanita the rest of the way. I'll hitch your horse to mine."

Cassie bristled. "I said I was fine. I'll ride alone."

Cole glared at her, his voice taking a sharp edge. "You'll ride with Juanita if I have to tie you to the damn saddle."

"Oh no," Juanita was quick to interject. "She is too heavy, and I cannot stop her if she falls again."

Cole let out a frustrated breath. "Fine," he said, his stalwart gaze matching Cassie's, "you ride with me."

He rose to prepare their horses, leaving Cassie glowering at him on the ground.

With a lending hand, Juanita assisted Cassie to her feet. "It is better this way, *si?*"

Cassie gave her friend a recriminatory stare. "Too heavy for you, huh? Oh, that's rich! When all you do is nag me about being too skinny."

"You are. But you are tall. Long bones are heavy," Juanita was quick to add.

Leading his horse by the reins, Cole stopped in front of them. "Hop on," he ordered Cassie.

She stared at the saddle. Her heart quickened at the thought of having to share that small space with the man. She'd be pressed up against him, wearing nothing but a duster and trousers. She didn't like this one bit.

Cole clucked his tongue with some impatience. "We're burnin' daylight here."

Sliding an exasperated look his way, Cassie swung into the saddle, sitting astride. Cole climbed in behind her, his arms encircling her to gather the reins. Cassie arched her spine, trying not to touch any part of him.

"Your back's gonna kill you if you plan on riding like that," he said, spurring the horse into an even lope.

"I'll be fine."

"Maybe for an hour," he said evenly. "You'll be singing a different tune after three or four."

Cassie couldn't argue with that. "Reckon you're right."

She leaned against the warm, solid mass of his chest. It was her turn to feel him stiffen. That brought a smile to her face. Why should she be the only one riding uncomfortably?

They rode for the greater part of the day, stopping to set up camp once they reached the San Pedro River. Cassie argued against it, wanting to cover as many miles as possible while the sun was still out. However, Cole insisted they needed to rest. Juanita agreed with him, complaining of hunger pains and dizziness. Cassie, therefore, had no choice but to capitulate. And now, sitting around the campfire with her spine feeling like it were made of needles and the pounding of her head echoing in her ears, she was glad she did.

"You all right?"

Lifting her head from her bent knees, Cassie looked up at Cole. Apparently, he'd taken ample advantage of the river. His face was clean-shaven, and his long hair dripped water from the ends curling below his collar. She studied the strong line of his jaw, the full lips, slightly parted as he waited for her reply. Good Lord, this was one fine-looking man.

"Just got a headache."

"Maybe you should lie down," he suggested. "I got extra blankets."

Cassie stood, drawing on her rapidly dwindling energy reserve to do so without any assistance. "Heavens, no! I need to wash," she blurted, inwardly recoiling at the look of compassion he gave her.

"Juanita's by the river bank, washing her hair for the third time, I reckon," he said.

Cassie rolled her eyes. "Knowing her, she's probably used up all the soap."

Without another word, Cole walked away.

Cassie frowned, wondering if she had unwittingly insulted him. He returned, offering her a white, square cake of castile soap. Cassie took it, and glanced at his hand, noticing the injured knuckles. Discolored and cut, it looked as if he'd smashed his hand against a brick wall. Before she could question him about it, he pulled it away.

"Best hurry before it gets dark," he said, tossing her a blanket as he marched away.

Cassie didn't need any urging. With soap and blanket in hand, she headed toward the river and found Juanita actively rinsing her hair. Upon seeing Cassie, she brought a hand to her mouth.

"Oh, *señorita,* I am so very sorry," she moaned, glancing remorsefully at the thin sliver of soap on the ground.

Cassie waved her white bar in the air. "I got plenty right here."

Juanita stood, glancing down at her sullied dress, her face pinched with disgust.

"Don't worry about the clothes, Juanita," Cassie said, eyeing the dreadful state of her own attire. "I'm sure Shillings has a decent dress shop."

Juanita picked at her clothes. "I still feel dirty with these on."

Cassie kicked off her pants and shrugged out of her chemise and shirtwaist, discarding the latter two into the river. She waded into the water, her skin prickled from the cold. "You don't know the meaning of the word," she said beneath her breath.

"You will catch your death, *señorita!*" Juanita yelled from the shore.

Ignoring Juanita's protests, Cassie dove into the river, her teeth chattering when she broke the surface. "I won't be long."

"Okay, but hurry. We must eat," Juanita called back, shaking her head as she stomped away.

After her bath, Cassie returned to the campfire. Hair dripping and body still shivering, she plopped on the ground beside Juanita. Cole sat across from her, his back against a boulder, forearms resting on his bent knees. Their eyes met over the fire. Cassie quickly looked away.

Juanita handed her a tin plate of beans, dried beef, and a sourdough biscuit. She wagged a finger in silent warning. "You have to eat it all."

Cassie did. She cleaned her plate, realizing how hungry she was when she took the first bite of her biscuit. Juanita also ate with gusto and later offered to clean up. Cole, however, didn't eat. He drank coffee, scanning the surroundings like he expected someone, or something to burst out of the darkness.

"You're not eating," Cassie remarked, the moment Juanita left with the dishes.

"Full stomach makes you groggy," he explained,

taking another sip of coffee. "Can't keep watch if I'm asleep."

Cassie looked all around, suddenly growing anxious. "What are you watching out for?"

"Everything."

"Oh," she said, feeling inept. That was a silly question.

Juanita returned, her presence ending their pithy exchange, and began preparing their respective sleeping arrangements. Cassie glanced longingly at her bedroll, her aching bones crying out for sleep. Then she looked at Cole, troubled by the shadows cradling his eyes. She felt like a heel, knowing she was the culprit of his unrest, realizing she had yet to thank him for saving their lives.

"Mr. Mitchell..."

As if he knew what was coming, and wanted no part of it, Cole stood up. He dusted the seat of his pants. "Try to get some sleep," he said, disappearing into the darkness beyond the light of the fire.

Chapter 10

Cole mashed his cigarette beneath the heel of his boot. He strode to the river, the walk soothing his cramped legs. He was tired. Bone tired to be exact. He splashed water in his face, its stinging chill chased the fatigue away.

Here he was, back on the trail, leaving a mighty fine salary behind, too. Not that he couldn't make money elsewhere. He usually made plenty of it whenever he chose, and he did have a substantial sum squirreled away. But Barrington must've figured out what went down by now, along with Ike's premature demise. The latter being the only good thing to come out of this whole filthy mess.

He studied his injured hand, images of Cassie, half-naked and bleeding, flashed in his mind. Raines and that mudsling were fixing to have their own private shindig. Lousy sons of bitches. He hadn't killed Ike, though he was certain he left him hanging by a thread. But what he couldn't finish, the fire did, and for that, he was grateful.

He was also angry with himself. If he'd only gotten to the barn sooner, Cassie would've never experienced the horror she did. He found some respite in the fact that she hadn't been violated in the literal sense, though he didn't know if that made any difference to her. The fright of it all was probably just as bad.

Behind him, he heard footsteps. From their distinct sound, he knew it was Cassie. She walked with a purpose, with valor in her step. And after all she'd been through. He felt an increasing sense of admiration for the woman.

"Mr. Mitchell?"

"Cole will do," he said, more irritably than he'd intended. "Don't think I'm that much older than you, so you can quit callin' me so proper like."

"How old are you?" she asked, catching him by surprise. He hadn't expected her to be particularly interested.

"By my last count, twenty-seven. Though I could be plumb off a year or two."

"You're right," she said. She took a moment to clear her throat as she nervously fingered the buttons on the duster she wore. *His duster.* "I got a couple of years on you."

Cole stared at her with some surprise. "Hell, woman, you don't look it."

Cassie shrugged. "I apologize for disturbing you. I got worried when you didn't return. And, I couldn't sleep, anyhow. Got too much on my mind."

Cole studied her profile, sketched with perfect detail, delicate, but strong. Her hair dried into thick, glossy waves, the ends curling at her waist. His fingers itched to sink into the silky mass, to pull her close, craving to feel her body against his. He couldn't believe he was lusting after a woman like this. Like he were a randy schoolboy again. Truth be told, it had been a while since his last good roll in the hay.

He forced his gaze to the river. "Well, try to get some shut-eye. You'll have plenty of time for frettin' once you're at Lil's."

"Lil's your sister?"

"Yep."

"Is she married?"

"Nope."

"Does she run the boarding house with your folks, then?" Cassie asked, staring at her boots.

"No," he replied, smiling at her sudden interest in his background. "Our folks passed on years ago."

"Oh," she said after a moment of silence. "I'm sorry. My ma passed on too, not long after I was born. Smallpox. Pa said I caught it soon after, but I lived through it."

He looked at her then, wanting to know as much about this confounding woman as he possibly could. "Folks say she was your pa's housekeeper?"

Cassie's chin lifted a proud peg. "At one time. But she was never his mistress. Pa said she was the church-going sort, and they were married right and proper years before I was born. Folks just didn't take to her, on account of her being Mexican and all."

"Your pa never remarried?"

Cassie shook her head, a melancholic smile lit her face. "He said no woman could ever take Ma's place. At the end..." she brushed a few errant curls from her face, "...the consumption took him quick, he didn't suffer like some."

Seeking to divert her sad thoughts Cole ventured, "And Juanita? She'd rather be with you than her kin?"

"Juanita's been with me over six years now. Pa hired her after Nacha, our original housekeeper, got married and moved to Carson City. Juanita was just thirteen then," Cassie said with a quiet laugh, "and already wise beyond her years. I've never met any of her kin. All I know is she's got her ma and grandma in Tijuana."

"She's mighty fond of you."

"She's my friend," Cassie said, kicking a pebble into the water. "I'd trust her with my life. Don't you have anybody you trust like that?"

Cole clenched his jaw. "No."

"How about your sister?"

"That's different, she's kin."

"Don't see how," Cassie said, furrowing her brow. "You can still be friends with your sister. And she must be of the first water to take in a couple of strangers."

Cole cupped her chin. "It's a boarding house, darlin'," she takes in strangers all the time," he teased, hoping to get another smile from her.

But she didn't smile. She just stared at him with those haunting emerald eyes brimming with fear, sorrow, and something else that slammed into his gut with the force of a freight train.

Desire.

She pulled his hand away and studied it beneath the moonlight. Her fingers traipsed along his injured knuckles. "This happened in my barn, didn't it?"

He breathed deeply. She smelled clean, of soap and river water. "Yeah," he whispered, lacing his fingers with hers. He tugged her hand until she stepped closer.

Cassie's eyes searched his face, stopping at his mouth. She leaned forward, his heart banged against his ribs as she closed her eyes, the tip of her nose touching his. But Cole didn't move-didn't crush her against him, or kiss her supple mouth, even though every fiber in his being wanted to. He couldn't take advantage of the situation they were in. Besides, he wanted her alert and willing, both physically and emotionally, not wounded and vulnerable like she was now.

His lack of response seemed to thwart her forward advance, and she drew back, blinking as if emerging from a spell.

"Good night, Mr. Mitchell," she said.

She hurried back, and left him alone by the river.

Chapter 11

Cassie trailed behind Juanita and Cole as they rode toward the mining town of Shillings. With bones that felt as brittle as glass, she shifted in her saddle, trying to ignore the simmering pain in her head. She sighed with relief when they passed the wooden, hand-painted welcome sign, indicating the town had a population of a 1,100 souls, no doubt seeking their respective fortunes in the dank belly of the silver mine.

Her eyes drifted to Cole, leading the way to the town's hub. To think she almost kissed him last night. She didn't know what had come over her. *Probably her physical exhaustion.* The desire to lean into him, to pilfer some of his strength, had been too strong. Acting on that need, she managed to make a total fool of herself. He never even tried to kiss her back. Why he just stood there like some marble statue, cold and unresponsive. He probably thinks her a loose trollop now, and she wouldn't blame him, either.

"*Señorita*, look," Juanita exclaimed with delight, pointing to the boardwalk the moment they turned onto Main Street, "a dress shop!"

With an acknowledging smile, Cassie inspected the various storefronts lining the covered boardwalk. The dress shop was a compact, square structure, wedged between a photography studio and a print press. All three establishments had identical whitewashed false fronts, the frilly, lace-embroidered curtains of the dress shop being its sole distinguishing attribute. At the end of the boardwalk was a large, brick-front saloon, a wooden plank sign squeaked on rusty hinges in the desert wind from its second floor balcony.

End of the Line Saloon and Dance Hall, Cassie mentally noted, smiling at the proprietor's wit.

"*Andale, señorita!*" Juanita shouted, waiting for her

at the corner of the intersecting street.

Loosening the reins, Cassie dug in her heels, prompting her mount to pick up the pace. She followed Juanita along a narrow side road, spotting Cole just a few feet ahead. Still on horseback, he waited for them in front of a light blue, colonial-style farmhouse. The white picket fence encircling the dual-story structure gleamed with a fresh coat of paint, as did the water well standing in the center of the neatly tended front yard.

"This is your sister's house, *eh señor?*" Juanita asked, stopping next to him.

"Yep," Cole replied.

Cassie reined her horse beside Juanita. She slid a furtive glance Cole's way as he dismounted, marveling at his stamina. The man moved with a fluid grace that was both compelling and powerful. He didn't even look any worse for wear, when blast his hide, she knew he was in desperate need of a full night's sleep. With brittle bones countering her every movement, Cassie slid off her saddle and followed Cole to the covered wraparound porch.

From behind her Juanita said, "This is very nice, *si?*"

"Very," Cassie agreed, admiring the roses blooming in oak box planters hanging from the front windows.

Cole raised a hand, poised to knock, when the front door swung open. A petite, young woman with flowing, blond hair and warm brown eyes, which lit up like firecrackers at the sight of Cole, rushed to embrace him.

"Cole!" She wrapped both arms around his neck, her yellow gingham skirt swirling around his legs.

Directly behind her another woman stepped outside. Just slightly shorter than Cassie, she was striking in appearance, with a delicate, heart-shaped face that framed large, brown eyes. Her lustrous, auburn hair was upswept into a stylish pompadour. With both hands stuffed into the front pockets of her checked walking skirt, she shook her head at the blond woman still dangling from Cole's neck.

"Honestly, Sylvia," she chastised, prying the young woman away, "let me hug my brother, will you?"

It took Sylvia a mighty long time to step away from Cole. The woman pouted when she finally did, leaning a shoulder against the doorframe as she stared at Cassie.

"New boarders?" she asked with a smirk. "I didn't know they were hiring womenfolk at the mine."

Cole gave her a scathing look. "That's enough, Sylvia."

"Where are my manners!" the taller and more well-mannered woman exclaimed. She turned to Cassie, her eyes widened as they explored her bruised face. "I'm Lillian Mitchell, Cole's sister. But folks call me Lil."

"Very nice to meet you, Lil." Cassie shook her extended hand. "I'm Cassie Taylor, and this is Juanita Gomez."

Juanita shook Lil's hand with a smile, and nodded a silent greeting at Sylvia, who failed to return the courtesy.

"That's Sylvia Vaughn," Lil motioned to the younger woman who was busy glaring at Cassie, "she's my cook and helps with the chores as well."

Cassie felt about as welcome as a tax collector with the way Sylvia eyeballed her, so she skipped the formalities, dismissing the churlish woman with a roll of her eyes.

"Sylvia, kindly see to the horses," Lil said, sending the petulant woman stomping down the porch steps. With a genial smile, she turned to Cassie. "Right this way."

Like an unseen drape the smell of pine oil hung thickly inside the entryway. Following Lil into the parlor, Cassie made a conscious effort to keep her boots from scratching the recently polished, wooden floors. Judging from the elegantly decorated surroundings, Cassie concluded Lil was doing mighty well for herself. Not too many folks could afford a matching upholstered parlor suite like the one arranged in front of the fireplace, complete with marble-top center table.

Lil joined Cole on the settee and gestured for Cassie and Juanita to take the sofa across from them. She was about to speak when Sylvia hurried into the room, making a beeline for Cole.

Before she could take a seat, however, Lil said, "Sylvia, be a dear and heat some water for a bath."

"Now that you mention it," Sylvia announced, eyeing both Cassie and Juanita with exaggerated revulsion, "that would be a wonderful idea." She marched out of the room, making quite a show of pinching her nostrils shut along the way.

Juanita looked at Cassie, her eyes round saucers of indignation. Cassie rolled a shoulder, indicating she could care less about the woman's petty affront.

Lil shook her head. "Don't mind her," she said to Cassie. "Sylvia takes some getting use to. She's not that bad once you get to know her."

Cassie gave her a perfunctory smile, watching Lil become a watery image before her eyes. She blinked, used her thumb and pointer finger to rub her eyelids.

Juanita elbowed her. "*Señorita*, are you all right?"

Lil rose from her seat. "Cole, wait here while I show the ladies to their rooms."

He nodded in silent reply.

Cassie caught the worried look he directed her way, perplexed as to its cause. She felt fine, just a might tired is all.

Juanita reached for her. "*Señorita*, come."

Taking Juanita's hand, Cassie followed her and Lil up the stairs to the second floor.

"You're in luck. My larger rooms vacated yesterday," Lil said, opening the door to the first room lining the long hallway. Looking at Juanita she asked, "Will this do?"

Juanita stepped inside, looking all around. "*Sí*, it is perfect,"

Lil smiled and handed Juanita a skeleton key from her skirt pocket. "Very well. It's all yours." She then guided Cassie to the room next door. "I think you'll be more comfortable here."

Cassie walked inside, immediately pleased with what she saw. A large, mahogany dresser filled the greater part of the right-hand wall. Perpendicular to it stood a matching vanity complete with oval mirror and upholstered bench. There was a full-size, brass-framed bed in the center of the room, covered with a blue-checkered quilt. Sheer lace curtains ornamented the two double-hung windows on the opposite wall, where a commode displayed a floral, porcelain washbowl and pitcher set.

"Like I was saying before, these rooms just vacated yesterday," Lil said. "We have the house to ourselves at the moment. So, you'll have plenty of peace and quiet."

Cassie perched on the edge of the bed, scrubbing her face with both hands. "I'm much obliged, Lil. I want you to know that I'll pay for both myself and Juanita. Though I can't just yet."

"There'll be plenty of time to discuss those arrangements later," Lil said. "Right now, just get some sleep."

Cassie nodded, talking was beginning to become too much of an effort as well.

"Let me take a look at that," Lil smoothed Cassie's hair from her brow. She leaned forward to inspect her wounds. "The cut on your forehead may leave a small scar."

Cassie studied Lil's pretty face, realizing both she and Cole shared the same whiskey-hued eyes. "Yes," she said, hoping Lil wouldn't question her about the events leading to her injuries. She was in no mood or condition to discuss them.

Lil seemed to understand Cassie's reticence. With a sympathetic smile, she turned toward the door.

"I'll be downstairs with Cole. Just holler if you need anything," she said, leaving the room key on the dresser top as she made her way out.

Expelling a deep breath, Cassie sagged against the mattress like a deflated balloon, falling asleep the moment her eyes closed. At one point, she thought someone tried to wake her. She felt hands on her, rubbing the length of her arms as if to warm her. Fingers caressed her face, smoothing her hair back. Then they were gone, and a part of her nebulous consciousness deemed it all just a dream as she drifted back to that sweet, beckoning void. It seemed only moments passed when the hands returned, shaking her shoulders none-too-gently.

"*Señorita*, wake up," Juanita's voice penetrated the darkness.

With a groan, Cassie sat up. The oil lamp glowing on the dresser spread a bright, shimmering light across the room.

"Most of the day," Juanita informed her.

"Damn," Cassie cursed, swinging her legs over the side of the bed.

74

A familiar pain assaulted her, and she cradled her throbbing head in her hands. She heard Juanita fumbling about at the commode.

"Here, take this." Juanita handed her a glass of water and a bottle of laudanum.

Cassie removed the cork top with her teeth. She poured some of the liquid into the glass, stirring it with one finger. Tossing her head back, she drained the contents and scrunched her face with its bitter taste.

"You put too much," Juanita said, taking the empty glass away.

"Once won't kill me." Cassie studied Juanita through narrowed eyes. "New get-up?" she asked, indicating the dark blue calico skirt and fitted bodice Juanita wore. She smelled like jasmines, and her freshly scrubbed face glowed like polished maple.

Juanita looked at her reflection in the vanity mirror. A satisfied grin cracking along her face. "It is *señorita* Lil's," she explained, redirecting her gaze to Cassie.

Cassie angled a brow in silent question. Lil was a good five inches taller than Juanita, and at least fifteen pounds heavier.

"I fixed it to fit me," Juanita said. "The skirt was too long. Why, *señorita* Lil is almost as tall as you, *mi patrona!*" she cried, as if that were an astonishing feat. She turned back to the dresser, bringing Cassie a stack of neatly folded clothes. "These are for you."

Cassie arranged the various garments on the bed. She pushed the chemises, bloomers, petticoats, and stockings to one side, pursing her mouth with displeasure when she saw the whale-boned corset.

"We're going to that dress shop first thing tomorrow, Juanita," she announced, running a hand over a blue-checkered gingham dress. "We'll get what we need and give Lil all her things back."

Juanita made an exasperated gesture. "It is rude to return a gift, *señorita*. I had to fix these clothes to fit me. I can not give it back now."

"Well, that's your choice. But I'm not keeping any of this." Cassie held the whale-boned corset by its laces. "I need a sturdy pair of trousers, and some work shirts. Hopefully, I can find some comfortable boots, too."

Juanita sighed. "I make all your clothes, *señorita*, remember? You will not find those things at a dress shop."

"What are you doing?" Cassie asked as Juanita rummaged through the dresser drawers.

"The bath is ready for you in the pantry. And look," she held out a sheer nightgown, "it is very nice, no?"

Cassie gaped at the flimsy, white nightdress. Sleeveless and sheer as an onionskin, with plunging neckline trimmed with lace, it served no practical purpose. With the scant coverage it provided, Cassie figured she might as well sleep unshucked.

"It most certainly is not nice, Juanita. Put it back."

"But this is for you. *Señorita* Lil said you could use whatever is in your room."

Cassie cast a sideward glance at the dresser. "Aren't there any others in there?"

Juanita shook her head. "No."

"Well, I suppose it'll have to do." Cassie tossed the nightgown on the bed. She turned at the sound of Juanita giggling.

"What's so funny?"

"*La bruja*," she explained with an impish wink. "*Señorita* Lil would not let her go home until she had your bath ready."

Cassie laughed. "Witch? You mean Sylvia. So she doesn't live here?"

"Oh, no. She lives with her *máma*. She works here during the day." Juanita grabbed Cassie's arm and dropped her voice to whisper, "I think she used to be the *señor's* woman."

Cassie stared at her and tried to sound disinterested. "Really?"

Juanita nodded her head. "She has no dignity, that one. She follows the *señor* everywhere like his shadow."

"Poor thing's smitten," Cassie said, engrossed by the clothing on her bed. She smoothed a few imaginary wrinkles from the gingham dress. "Why did you say '*use to be*'? She's not his woman now?"

"Oh no. I know these things, *si*? It is easy to see when a man wants a woman. He does not want her. Not anymore."

Cassie rolled a shoulder. "Reckon that's his affair, not

ours," she said, though she secretly wondered what Cole ever saw in that scrawny, plain-faced sourpuss. Why, she looked like she'd been weaned on a pickle, and she was about as tall as a June bug to boot.

"She tried to follow him in here."

Cassie snapped her head to stare at Juanita. "Here, in my room?"

"*Si*, when the *señor* came to check on you." Juanita shook her head. "But he would not let her come inside."

Cassie's heart hammered frantically, crashing against her ribs like a trapped bird as she recalled the hands smoothing her hair, the fingers on her face. Clearing her throat, she asked, "He tried to wake me before?"

Juanita's brow furled. "Not wake you, only check on you. He came downstairs and told us you were well, and to let you sleep."

"Oh, funny..." Cassie lied, swaying when she turned to the commode, "...I don't remember a thing."

She reached for a towel, feeling more lethargic with each passing moment. Her headache had miraculously vanished, and she felt a warm, tingling sensation, like invisible feathers sweeping along the length of her limbs. Maybe she had put a bit too much laudanum in that water.

"I could use a good scrubbing," she said through a forced smile, "show me to the bath, Juanita."

"Follow me." Juanita grabbed the gingham dress off the bed and led the way to the kitchen.

Cassie floated behind her. She was certain her feet never touched the ground, because she couldn't feel them. She also failed to notice when Juanita stopped to open the pantry door. Cassie crashed into her, and grabbed Juanita's arm to keep from toppling over.

"Oops, sorry."

Juanita eyed her intently. "*Señorita*, are you feeling well?"

"Of course."

Finding her balance, Cassie stepped inside. Her eyes strayed to the tin, oblong tub in the center of the pantry, steam rising from the perfumed bathwater in smoky curled ribbons. A wire soap dish holding a white, square cake hung over the rim. Beside the tub was a wooden pail with clean rinsing water and a small tin bowl.

"You should not have taken so much laudanum. What if you fall asleep and drown in the tub? *Madre Santa*," Juanita sighed, reaching for the towel in Cassie's hand. Neatly folding it, she placed it beside the gingham dress on a wooden, corner stool. "Do not worry. I will stay to help you."

Cassie shook her head. "Don't be silly. I'm fine, Juanita. Go on, now," she ordered, giving Juanita's shoulder a gentle shove. "I promise to call you if I need anything."

"You promise?"

Cassie fingered an invisible X over her heart. "I swear it."

Juanita turned away with some reluctance. "Very well. But if you take too long, I will come for you."

The sound of the door closing barely registered in Cassie's mind as she stripped out of her sullied garments. She jumped into the wooden tub and water splashed over the rim. Grabbing the soap, she lathered her hair, consuming a large part of the rinsing water on that task alone. A yelp escaped her when she washed her face and touched the temporarily forgotten gash on her temple. The image of Ike's snarling face leaning over her flashed before her eyes, and her stomach knotted in response. She began to scrub every inch of her flesh harder, leaving red fingernail tracks on her skin. She scrubbed until she was raw, her skin red, and she panted from her own violent exertions.

Leaning against the raised back of the tub, Cassie wiped tears from her eyes. The unexpected creak of the floorboards startled her, and she spun around, covering her breasts instinctively. *Good Lord, how long had he been standing there?* She hadn't even heard the door open.

"Sorry, didn't know anybody was here."

Cassie thought Cole's voice was about an octave lower. He turned around, speaking to her over his shoulder.

Stepping out of the tub, she wrapped the towel around her torso. "Ever heard of knocking?"

"I did," he said in his characteristic, lazy drawl.

"Twice."

"Well, I didn't hear you." She pulled the gingham dress over her head.

"Then you must be losing your hearing," he replied, his voice a high-pitched imitation of hers.

"I assure you that I'm not." Cassie straightened the dress as best she could, a difficult task given her damp skin. "But please, don't let me hold you up," she said as she marched by him.

Cole grabbed her arm and pulled her back. "What happened?" He stared at the red marks on her neck, exposed by her unbuttoned collar.

Cassie's entire body tingled with the way his eyes strayed from her neck, to her shoulders, to her breasts. She suddenly felt very vulnerable, the numbing effect of the laudanum dissipated with every breath she took.

"N-nothing," she said. "The water was too hot."

His eyes locked with hers, and she felt a longing in the pit of her stomach she'd never known before. She felt alive, like her body burned from the inside out, and a deep ache settled somewhere in her womb. An ache she intuitively knew only he could allay.

"I have to go," she said, without making the slightest attempt to leave.

He was so close, his face just inches from hers. She leaned into him, breathed in his familiar scent.

He coiled an arm around her waist. "No you don't."

Slowly, he dipped his head, and his lips skimmed hers. Cassie closed her eyes, her body quivered, despite the heat he stoked within her. She cursed her own weakness around this man. How she would melt, like butter in the sun, beneath his slightest touch.

Just like Sylvia probably did.

She fought the image of him holding Sylvia as he was holding her now. His eyes filled with passion, those full lips inviting, a sweet nepenthe for her battered soul.

With a surprising show of strength, she placed both hands flat against his chest and shoved him away. He looked at her, a mixture of confusion and surprise flickering in those whiskey eyes. She closed the gap between them and slapped him sharply across the face.

"Don't take such liberties with me, Mr. Mitchell."

Cassie dashed out the door before he could react. Afraid if she stayed, he'd see right through her farce, and kissed her until she was dizzy.

The way she really wanted him to.

Dry Moon

Chapter 12

It turned out Juanita was right. There were no trousers at Miss Prudence's Dress Shop, aptly named after its sole proprietor and attendant, Miss Prudence Opperman. Not to mention linen shirts, and after seeing the look of utter dismay flushing the deeply lined face of the elderly Miss Prudence, Cassie didn't bother inquiring about a good pair of work boots, either.

A frown puckered her lips as Cassie observed herself in the full-length mirror. The stylish, maroon day dress was comfortable enough. However, she wasn't too fond of its accompanying pillbox hat complete with ostrich feather perched low on her forehead. She removed the ostentatious thing and handed it to Lil.

"I don't think this one suits me," Cassie said.

"I think you look beautiful, *señorita*," Juanita said, engaged by her own reflection in the mirror. She wore a floral calico dress with flouncing white hem. "You like this one, no?" she asked Cassie.

"It's mighty fancy, if you ask me," Cassie mumbled as she struggled with the buttons on her bodice.

Circling Juanita, Lil said, "I think you look lovely."

Miss Prudence, who insisted on being called just that, put on the wire spectacles hanging on her neck from a silver chain. She smoothed her thinning, silver hair with both hands, patted the bun at the nape of her neck.

"Well, I'm sorry you can't seem to find something you like, dear," she said, loosening the laces of Cassie's corset. "I pride myself for having a mighty decent selection to choose from. Better than most 'round these parts."

"Oh, you do, Miss Prudence," Cassie said. Finally liberated of the corset choking the air from her lungs, she let out a deep sigh, and ducked behind the dressing screen. "I'm just looking for something more practical. I don't need any fancy get-ups."

81

"How about a riding skirt?" Lil suggested.

"All right," Cassie said, giving in a little.

Lil draped a skirt over the screen top. "This one should do."

A moment later, Cassie emerged wearing a simple, dark green split skirt and white embroidered shirtwaist. She frowned, wondering why all three women stared at her with silly grins on their faces. "I look ridiculous, don't I?"

"Not at all," Lil was quick to reply. "It's very becoming."

"*Si*, you look beautiful," Juanita agreed.

"If you wish," Miss Prudence said with a resounding sigh, "I can place a mail order for those items you first requested." From behind her wire spectacles, rheumy blue eyes assessed Cassie's figure. "They'll be men's clothes, mind you. You are rather tall, and the small sizes just might fit you with some minor alterations. If I place the order today, it should get here in a couple of weeks."

"That'd be wonderful," Cassie said. "I'll leave you a list."

"And what you're wearing now?" Lil asked her.

Glancing down at her outfit, Cassie shrugged. "It'll do."

Miss Prudence sighed with relief. "Thank the good Lord."

After leaving an extensive mail order, the women left the store.

"*Diosito*, I feel so much better now with new clothes!" Juanita cried, climbing into Lil's surrey.

Cassie scooted to the middle of the bench to make room for her friend. "I appreciate you letting me use your credit with Miss Prudence," she said to Lil sitting at the reins. "I'll pay you back as soon as I can."

"No need to thank me. I'm glad to help." With a slap of the reins, Lil set the surrey in motion.

Cassie looked at the various shops along the boardwalk. "Is there a post office in town, Lil?"

"Why, yes. It opened last summer. It's on Second Avenue, just a couple of streets behind us," she said, gesturing in that direction. "Asa Johnson is the postmaster, and he owns the mercantile next door to it."

She chuckled, shaking her head as she added, "Asa and Miss Prudence go at it like cats and dogs. Yet one can't live without visiting the other on a daily basis. But believe me, whatever you need you will find at Asa's Mercantile."

"Even a gun?"

"A gun?" Lil repeated with a frown.

"Yeah. A good one, not them little derringers they sell women."

"You can definitely see Asa about that, too. I keep a Winchester, myself," Lil added. "Cole taught me how to shoot."

"We are very grateful to the *señor*," Juanita said. "He saved our lives."

"Yes, Cole told me what happened." Lil said, her tone was hushed. "I'm very sorry for your loss."

Cassie kept her blank stare rooted on the passing scenery. "So am I."

"Although, I must confess I admire you," Lil said. "Running a business is a difficult thing. Especially one that doesn't take too kindly to women."

"*Mi patrona* is a very good business woman." Juanita came to her defense. "And she can shoot better than any man."

"For all the good that did us," Cassie mumbled.

"But we are alive." Taking Cassie's hand, Juanita gave it a gentle squeeze. "We are very lucky."

"You are both very fortunate, indeed," Lil agreed.

As if on cue, Cassie's head began a rhythmic throbbing. She closed her eyes, willing the pain away.

Lil pulled up to the boarding house. A worry line etched along her brow when she looked at Cassie. "Is it your head again?"

Cassie nodded, relieved to be home.

"Come," Lil said. With a supporting arm, she helped Cassie step down from the buggy. "Some laudanum will take care of that."

"And some food," Juanita added, following both women into the house.

The site of Sylvia waiting for them in the entry hall only served to exacerbate the pounding between Cassie's temples.

"Hello, Sylvia," Lil greeted her employee.

Sylvia's reply was an annoyed 'hmph'.

Lil frowned. "What's the matter?"

"The note you left me said you'd be back early." Though Sylvia addressed Lil, her dark eyes were rotted on Cassie.

"Sorry about that," Lil apologized. "We were delayed at Miss Prudence's."

The apology failed to mollify the sullen young woman. "Well, while you were dallying with the boarders, I finished the laundry and had breakfast on the table. It got cold since nobody bothered to show up..." She sighed, adding a slump of her shoulders to her meretricious pout, "...or bothered to tell me they wouldn't be showing up."

Lil shook her head. "Well, how's about I make it up to you?"

"Don't see how you can," Sylvia mumbled, folding both arms across her chest.

"Well, how's about you go home early today?" Lil suggested with a smile. "I'll finish up whatever needs to be done."

The pout she'd been milking vanished from Sylvia's face with remarkable swiftness. "Leave early?" she said with an edgy chuckle. "Oh no, that just won't be possible. I still have to wash the windows. Lunch and supper have to be prepared and-"

"Oh, but I can cook, *señorita* Lil," Juanita said.

"Nonsense. You're my guest. I can't rightly put you to work."

"But I like to cook, *señorita*, I really do," Juanita insisted. She turned to Cassie for support. "Tell her, *señorita*."

"Let her cook, Lil," Cassie said. "She loves it, and she's damn good at it too."

Sylvia snorted with disapproval. Glaring at Cassie she declared, "Women shouldn't cuss."

Cassie smiled sweetly in return. "And you learned this at your finishing school for uppity maids and such?"

Juanita coughed, stifling a laugh when Sylvia's face bloomed crimson.

"All right now." Lil was quick to interrupt, the tone of her voice broached no rebuttal. "Juanita will do the cooking today. Sylvia you start on the windows."

With another roll of her eyes, Sylvia turned to leave. "At least Cole enjoyed my breakfast," she said, giving Cassie a smug grin as she sauntered by her.

Well, bully for you. Cassie's eyes stabbed into Sylvia's retreating back.

"Allow me to apologize for Sylvia," Lil said. "She took a cotton to my brother years ago, and it brings out the worst in her, I'm afraid."

"She used to be his woman?" Juanita asked, giving Cassie an 'I told you so' look.

"Something like that," Lil replied. Without elaborating further, she turned to look at Juanita. "You sure you don't mind cooking, Juanita?"

"No, *señorita*," she said. "I will make something so good, you will lick your fingers."

"Well, if you insist," Lil relented. She led Juanita by the arm. "Follow me, I'll show you around the kitchen."

Cassie walked in the opposite direction toward the stairwell, massaging her throbbing temples. "I'm gonna lie down for a spell."

"Oh, my goodness, your laudanum." Lil smacked a hand against her forehead. "Go to my room, Cassie. It's just at the end of the hall. The door's unlocked, and there's a new bottle on the commode."

Cassie took her time ascending the stairs. Like an orchestra conductor, each step seemed to set off a different drum pounding in her head. At the second floor landing, she stopped to massage her temples before proceeding down the corridor.

There were two rooms at the very end. One had its door slightly ajar. Cassie pushed it open and stepped inside, frowning at the rather austere décor. The walls were papered with an indigo and white pinstripe pattern. A dark brown smoking chair with rawhide throw draped over its arm stood wedged between an oak dresser and the windowsill. The double-sized, four-poster bed was made up with plain white sheets pulled taut over the mattress like a drum skin. It was a room better suited for a man, she thought as she glanced toward the commode beside the bed. Aside from the white porcelain bowl and pitcher, there was nothing on its marble-top surface.

"Fancy finding you here."

Startled by the sound of Cole's voice, Cassie spun on her heel. She braced a tremulous hand on the bedpost to keep her balance.

"I-I'm sorry, I-"

"Some advice, darlin'," he drawled, in that patronizing fashion she was becoming familiar with, "before snooping, always lock the door."

Producing a set of keys from his back pocket, Cole did just that.

Cassie heard the lock snap into place, and her heart leapfrogged into her throat.

With arms folded across his chest, Cole leaned against the door to stare at her. "Not so hard, is it?" he asked, a lazy grin lifting one corner of his mouth.

Cassie struggled to maintain eye contact. Suddenly, the pounding of her heart outpaced the one in her head. Her mouth felt like she'd just dined on cotton and parchment paper. Why did the mere sight of this man unravel her so? Somehow, she felt as if his presence made the room smaller, made *her* feel smaller, and very vulnerable. He was just too...too...*male*. She could see the chiseled contours of his torso through his white, linen shirt. Snug, brown trousers delineated the muscles of his long legs, flaring at the heel to accommodate his spurs. Cassie's gaze slid to his gun belt, riding low on his slim hips. A stark reminder of how this man made his living. Lean and sleek, he looked at her with a hunter's prowess, as if testing her resolve. If she wanted to leave, she'd have to get through him first.

"I wasn't snooping," she said, and then cleared her dry throat. "I needed some laudanum, and I thought this was Lil's room."

He jerked a thumb to the opposite wall. "Her room's next door."

"Oh, then if you'll pardon me," Cassie said, taking a measured step toward the door.

She waited for him to move aside, but he appeared in no hurry to accommodate her. He just stood there, his whiskey eyes assessing her wardrobe.

"You're all gussied up today."

"I'm not gussied up." Her patience snapped like a dry

86

twig. "And could you please let me by?"

With a mocking tip of his hat he complied. "All you had to do was ask."

Cassie made a beeline for the door. Her fingers like jittery spider legs fumbled with the key he left in the lock. She stiffened when she felt Cole walk up behind her.

"Your head aching again?"

The genuine concern in his voice beckoned her to face him, and she turned, flattening her back against the door when she realized how close he was.

"Yes," she said, unable to suppress the tremors that rippled through her body when he braced a hand on the door, preventing her departure.

"Listen," he began, those whiskey eyes darkening as he spoke, "I apologize about last night. I was outta line."

Cassie felt the blood drain from her face. She gaped at him, wondering if this bout of remorse had anything to do with one presumptuous, love-struck maid. Her pride cracked like an ice chip with that thought, and she squared her shoulders.

"Honestly, Mr. Mitchell, you don't really believe I gave that a second thought, do you?"

A muscle rolled along the firm line of his jaw, the only emotional indicator Cassie could perceive from his otherwise stony expression. Reaching around her, he pulled the door open, forcing Cassie to stumble forward.

"Next time, make sure you knock first," he said.

With a caustic smile, Cassie marched out of his room. Though she felt his heavy gaze on her back, she didn't bother looking over her shoulder when she said, "Rest assured, there *won't* be a next time."

Chapter 13

Barrington walked into the foreman's cabin and ordered Rosa out with a jerk of his head. Hobbling around the wooden bed, the old healer gathered her belongings, stuffing an assortment of leaves and herbs into her buckskin medicine bag.

"All is good, *patron*," she informed him on her way out.

Barrington approached the bed. "You look like shit, Ike," he said, studying his range boss' swollen, battered face.

"I feel like it, too." Ike carefully fingered the cotton strip covering his right eye. "I'm gonna get Mitchell for this."

Barrington glowered at him. "Ya ain't gonna do nothin' but lay low for now, got that? You were damn lucky to have crawled out of that barn with your hide still in one piece. You left a trail, Ike." He shook his head. "One that leads straight to me. Now I gotta clean your mess up."

Raines swallowed hard. "Don't worry, boss. Them guns weren't from around these parts. Nobody can tie 'em to us."

"I don't care about them. Dead men can't talk." Barrington couldn't believe the stupidity of his range boss. "I'm worried about the live ones that got away. You're an idiot, Ike!"

"I wasn't countin' on Mitchell showing up," Raines said. "I told ya he'd turn on you, didn't I? Somebody snitched, boss. Somebody on this here spread!"

"Yeah," Barrington mumbled more to himself than to Ike. "Got me a rat to find."

"We gotta find that bitch first," Raines said.

"You don't say?" Barrington stabbed at him with a chubby finger. "And just what the hell ya think I been doin' for that past two days, you jackass?"

Raines stared at his lap. "Sorry, boss."

There was a soft knock on the door, followed by Katherine's lyrical voice. "Amos?"

Letting out an exasperated breath, Barrington opened the door to glare at his wife. "What is it now, woman? I'm busy."

Katherine took a guarded backward step. "I-I'm sorry to disturb you, Amos," she said. "But the sheriff is here. He says he needs to talk to you."

"He does, does he?" Barrington tossed Raines a virulent look over his shoulder.

"Will you see him?" Katherine asked.

"In a minute." Barrington closed the door on his wife's face. Turning to Ike, he said, "Ya see what I gotta deal with on account of your blundering?"

"He ain't got nuthin' on us," Ike said. "You'll see."

Barrington licked his lips. "And I'm gonna make sure it stays that way."

****

Sheriff Brady waited in the sitting room. Recognizing the sound of Katherine's light footsteps, he rose just as she opened the pocket doors. "Ma'am."

"Thank you for waiting, Sheriff," she said. "Amos will only be a moment. I apologize for not asking before, but your visit caught me by surprise. Would you care for some coffee?"

He smiled. "That's mighty nice of you ma'am, but no thank you."

Brady held her gaze, fascinated by the honey and olive kaleidoscope of her eyes. He thought the embarrassed flush of her cheeks made her even more beautiful.

Katherine let out a small, nervous laugh. "Of course you don't want coffee, it's so dreadfully hot out, isn't it?"

"That it is, ma'am."

He watched her twirl her wedding band around her finger. "Then how about some lemonade, instead?" she offered. "I just made some this morning."

"I'm sure it's delicious." He couldn't keep from staring into those clear, honey-colored eyes. "But I'm fine, thank you."

After an awkward silence, Katherine finally said, "Well, I-I have dishes in the sink."

"Don't let me keep you, ma'am," Brady said, admiring once again the return of color to her cheeks.

"Howdy there, Sheriff." Like a skunk's stench, Barrington's voice filled the room. "To what do I owe the pleasure?"

Brady glared at the rotund man. "We need to talk, Amos."

"Of course." He placed a fleshy hand on Brady's shoulder. "Come, my office is down the hall." Turning to his wife, Barrington demanded, "Did you offer the good man here something to drink?"

"She did," Brady was quick to intercede, "I graciously declined."

"Well then, just follow me," Barrington said, leading the way to the library.

Inside, he gestured for Brady to have a seat. "You sure you don't want anything to drink, Sheriff? I got the good stuff in here, you know."

Taking the empty seat across the mahogany desk, Brady removed his hat, and raked a hand through his hair. "No, I'm fine, Amos."

"All right." Barrington took his own seat. Like a reverential pupil, he folded his hands, rested them on the desktop. "So, what's this we need to talk about?"

"Cassie Taylor." Brady scrutinized the cattle baron's face, unable to find even an inkling of emotion. "Seems she's gone missing."

"Missing?" Barrington furled his pink brow, as if genuinely confused.

"That's right," Brady said, his level gaze spearing the older man. "Miller fetched me early this morning. Seems he stopped by the Taylor spread to pay his dues and found the entire place burnt to a crisp."

"Burned down!" Barrington placed a hand over his heart. "How?"

Brady could've done without the theatrics. "The *how's* the easy part. It's the *who* that's a might trickier. Got me a heap of bodies out there, so burned up it was quite a task telling 'em apart. Though, I could identify Villanueva by his shot up hand..." Brady gave him a wry grin, "...and

90

I could tell none of 'em were female."

"T-this is horrible news, Sheriff."

"A downright filthy mess is what it is," Brady corrected.

Barrington shook his head. "What's this world comin' to when a woman ain't safe in her own home?"

"Don't recall you caring much about Miss Taylor's welfare before, Amos," Brady said, winging a dark brow.

"It's true, we had our differences." Barrington seemed to bristle beneath the sheriff's stare. "But that don't mean I wished her any personal misfortune. I'm a God-fearing man, after all."

Brady had to admit, it was hard to tell when the man was lying. "So, you're sayin' you don't know anything about this?"

"I ain't no killer," Barrington avowed. "And I'd appreciate it if you quit insulting me in my own house."

"That'd be a no?"

Barrington shot to his feet. "Of course it is! I'll have you know that I've been in this town longer than you've been alive. Ain't no law 'round here back then, and decent men like myself were forced to deal with the unsavory fellers up to no good. I made sure this town was safe for honest, hard working folks. You got no right treatin' me like I'm some low-down chiseler!"

"Pipe down, Amos," Brady said, not at all impressed by the cattle baron's tirade. "I'm fixin' to talk to all the members on the board, if it makes you feel any better. I came here first on account of your *strained* relationship with Miss Taylor," he said. "Folks in this town hired me to do a job, and that's all I'm tryin' to do. Your cooperation would be appreciated."

With a grunt, Barrington reclaimed his seat. "Well, I got no problem cooperatin' with the law." Reaching for a silk kerchief in his front pocket, he blotted sweat from his reddened face. "I've worked mighty hard at making a good name for myself. Reckon I'm a might protective of it, is all."

"Can't blame a man for that."

"But I don't know nuthin' about this nasty business," Barrington continued. "That's the honest-to-God truth. And you can just go on and question every man on this spread if you feel the need to."

"That won't be necessary," Brady said with an appeasing smile. "Don't think they'll tell me any different."

Barrington snorted. "Only 'cos there ain't nuthin' more to tell."

Brady observed him a moment. Though his instincts told him otherwise, there was no evidence linking Barrington to what happened at the Taylor Ranch. He couldn't very well accuse the man on a hunch, either. "Well, I appreciate your time, Amos." He rose and re-donned his hat. "I got some more rounds to make today, so I'll just be on my way."

Barrington remained seated. It was clear to Brady he'd have to see himself out. "Well, I'm sorry I couldn't be of more help to ya, Sheriff."

Brady bristled at the smug tone. In retaliation, he chose to leave the man with a gnawing doubt. "You got it all wrong," he said with a smile. "You've been mighty helpful."

Closing the door on the frowning cattle baron, Brady strode down the corridor. From behind him, a faint sound caught his ear. He stopped to look over his shoulder. Honing his senses, he thought he saw something move at the opposite end of the hall.

With a hand on his gun holster, Brady headed in that direction. He discovered Katherine hiding in the corner. Given her strategic location beside the library, it was obvious she'd been eavesdropping on her husband. Brady had a feeling this wasn't the first time, either. She huddled against the wall, shoulders slumped, as if trying to submerge within the shadows.

Brady closed in on her, his tall form casting a shadow that swallowed her whole. "Ma'am?"

Katherine shook her head. Her wide eyes beseeched him. The fear he saw in their golden depths clawed at his stomach with steel talons.

With a nod signaling his understanding, Brady backed away. "You know where to find me."

Chapter 14

Stepping into the post office, Cassie's jingling spurs drew the attention of the dark-haired man standing behind a wooden counter.

"Howdy," the man greeted, pushing the journal he'd been writing in to one side. "How can I help you?"

"Good day," Cassie said. "I need to telegraph Encanto."

The man pushed the round spectacles up the bridge of his prominent nose. His brown eyes studied her from behind the lenses. From the smile he gave her, Cassie wasn't certain whether he was pleased or amused by what he saw. Perhaps a combination of the two.

"Then you came to the right place, little lady. The name's Asa Johnson."

Given the receding hairline peppered with silver along his broad temples, and deep lines fanning the corner of his eyes, Cassie assumed Mr. Johnson was somewhere in his late-fifties. But his broad, sturdily built frame belied his age by at least a decade.

Cassie shook the strong hand he offered. "Cassie Taylor."

"It's a pleasure to make your acquaintance, ma'am."

"Likewise."

"Let's see now," he said, producing a blank Western Union telegram pad from beneath the counter. Tearing off a sheet, he handed it to her. "Here you go. Just write down what you gotta say there, and I'll do the rest."

Cassie jotted down a brief message, and returned the form to Mr. Johnson. She waited while he sat at the telegraph machine and went about transforming her written words into a series of rapid clicks on the metal plate and sounder. Once finished, he made a notation in his journal and returned her handwritten form.

"You can keep that for your records."

"I'm staying at Miss Mitchell's boarding house, and she said you could add this to her account."

"Any friend of Lil's is a friend of mine," Mr. Johnson said with a friendly wink.

"Much obliged." Cassie glanced curiously around the room. "Also, I'm looking to purchase a gun."

"Is that so?" he said. "Then right this way, little lady."

Cassie followed him through a connecting side door into the mercantile. A young woman with fiery, shoulder-length curls sat at the attendant's desk, reading a dime novel. Apparently too engrossed by the story, she failed to acknowledge their presence until Mr. Johnson made it a point to clear his throat rather loudly.

"Oh, pardon me." The redhead folded the page she was reading in half before putting the book away.

"Marybeth, this is Miss Cassie Taylor," he said. "She's a friend of Lil's."

Doe-like, brown eyes inspected Cassie for a brief moment. "Hello," Marybeth greeted, two dimples piercing her freckled cheeks.

Cassie returned the young woman's genial smile. "Hello."

"Marybeth's my daughter-in-law," Mr. Johnson explained. "She helps me out around the store when she can spare the time, and she's a right fine telegraph operator, too."

"I had a good teacher," Marybeth said, wiggling her eyebrows at Cassie.

The older man blushed. "You go on back to your reading, Beth. I'll take care of Miss Taylor."

With a departing smile at the younger woman, Cassie followed Mr. Johnson to the opposite end of the store, where a variety of firearms were displayed inside a glass cabinet. Just as she expected, he grabbed one of the derringers, the dainty gun all but disappeared in his large hand.

"Now, this here's a fine little pistol."

"Actually," Cassie eyed the more lethal revolvers on the shelf, "I need something with more firepower. Like that one right there." She tapped a finger against the glass.

Putting the derringer back in its place, Mr. Johnson handed her the Colt Peacemaker she indicated. "Well, if it's firepower you want, then that's definitely the gun for it."

Cassie scrutinized every detail of the revolver. Palming it, she gauged its weight, then aimed at an imaginary target on the opposite wall. She fired an empty shot, listening to the hollow click of the hammer. Satisfied, she twirled the revolver on her index finger, holstering it with expert precision. "I'll take it."

Mr. Johnson gaped at her. "Y-yes, very good then." He handed her a box of ammunition. "Reckon you want me to add this to Lil's account as well?"

Cassie nodded. "And about that telegram, I'll be expecting-"

"Don't you fret none," he cut in. "I don't know if Lil's told you how we work around here, but we just got that telegraph machine few months back. This being a small town and all, well, we can't rightly afford any messenger boys. So either me or Marybeth deliver the telegrams ourselves. Though that depends on how busy we are." Mr. Johnson scratched his balding head. "Sometimes we wait until after we close up to deliver 'em. Of course, folks awaiting any urgent news and such are partial to checking in with me during the day. I'm here from eight to four, except on Sundays, of course."

Cassie gave him a farewell nod. "I'll do that, much obliged."

Outside, she gathered her horse at the hitching post. Sitting astride in the saddle, she rode down Main Street. Several women walking along the boardwalk, clad in colorful dresses and sunbonnets, stared at her. A few pointed her out, their fingers stabbing the open air to some article of clothing she wore, either her pants, or her boots with spurs, or her gun belt.

Pulling her Stetson low on her brow, Cassie spurred the horse to quicken the pace. *Nosy old windbags.* Such petty antics weren't going to dampen her good spirits, the result of Miss Prudence's impromptu visit earlier in the day. Cassie hadn't expected her mail order to arrive for at least another week, and was delighted Miss Prudence made the extra effort of personally hand delivering it. As expected, Juanita made her displeasure evident, pouting and shaking her head when Cassie emerged from her room in a pair of denim pants, linen shirt, and brown, leather boots. Lil offered no comment, aside from asking Cassie if her order was complete, and cutting Sylvia's guffaw short with a sharp jab of her elbow. Cole, on the other hand, had yet to see her.

Preferring to pass the time gallivanting at the saloon, he usually left early in the morning, and returned late in the evening, if he returned at all, that is. On those rare occasions when he did, the sound of his footsteps, heavy and uneven from all that rotgut, always managed to awaken her. What he did with his life was none of her affair. She had plenty of her own problems.

As she rounded the corner of the End of the Line Saloon, her rambling thoughts screeched to a halt. There, stepping out through its swinging doors, was the man in question himself. He wasn't alone. Resentment bubbled in her gut as she watched Sylvia lead Cole by the hand into a side alley. They never even glanced in her direction.

Cassie considered just moseying on home. She shouldn't really care what Cole and Sylvia were up to back there. But another part of her did care. Too much. Anticipation hitched her breath in her throat, and despite her better judgment, she turned around. After leaving her horse in a secluded spot by the livery, Cassie dashed across the street. As she neared the alleyway, her heart galloped in her chest like a wild stallion. Though she chided herself to the contrary, she was unable to refrain from peeking around the corner. She saw Cole and Sylvia at the far end, next to the stairs leading to the saloon's second floor. One look at the two of them, and Cassie realized she didn't have to hide. With the way they kissed, they wouldn't have noticed a stampeding herd barreling by them.

Aghast, she turned away. Why did it bother her so? Why couldn't she just get that blasted man out of her mind? He was like a sickness she couldn't rid herself of. With her conflicting emotions playing havoc on her stomach, Cassie hurried back to the livery. She mounted her horse, and took off without a backward glance.

****

Cole shoved Sylvia aside.

"Quit playing games." He wiped his mouth with the back of his hand. "Is this what you brought me out here for?"

"You never complained before," Sylvia said with an impish grin.

Cole turned away. "Hell, woman, you're like a burr in my saddle."

"Wait," Sylvia cried, chasing after him. When he didn't stop, she circled him, and blocked his path. "Wait, please. I really did need to talk to you," she said in a half-cajoling voice.

Cole eyed her warily. His gut told him to skedaddle out of there and pronto. But Sylvia usually screeched like a plucked jaybird when she didn't have her way, and he preferred to avoid any unsavory confrontation with her, especially in public.

"Then talk, but make it fast."

Sylvia stepped closer and fingered the buttons of his vest. "Please don't be cross with me, Cole." She continued in the same sugary tone, "It's just that you're hardly around anymore. I'm starting to think you're trying to avoid me."

"You're talking foolish."

Sylvia met his hard stare. "Am I?"

Cole pulled her hands away. "Yes, you are. Now, if you'll excuse me..."

He got as far as the boardwalk, almost breathed in a sigh of relief, too, until Sylvia marched in front of him, both hands on her hips.

"Don't you walk away from me," she hissed. "You think I don't see what's going on? You really think I'm that stupid, don't you?"

"I don't think anything, Sylvia," Cole said. "That's the point. I don't think about you at all."

"It's because of her, isn't it?" she demanded, stabbing a finger into his chest.

Cole shouldered her aside. "I don't know what you're talking about."

"Oh, you most certainly do know what I'm talking about," she shadowed his every step, "I see how you look at her. What is it about her that you find so appealing? Is it the cussing? Or the stench of horses? Or maybe the calluses on her hands?"

Cole didn't respond. Unable to control the anger simmering in his blood, he quickened his step, his long strides ate the ground like a hungry monster.

"I won't let you make a fool of me!" Sylvia shrieked behind him.

"Don't need to." Cole turned to face her. "You're doing a mighty fine job all on your own."

Sylvia clamped her lips together, her cheeks flared like crimson mushroom caps when she looked around, as if suddenly aware she stood in the middle of a bustling boardwalk. She met the reproaching gazes of several people walking by, and plucked her chin up.

"Let them stare," she said with a roll of her shoulder. "I've got nothing to hide. You're the one lusting after a woman who thinks she's a man."

Cole closed the gap between them. "Stay the hell away from me, Sylvia," he said, his voice barely above a whisper. "Get it through that thick head of yours." He tapped her forehead with two fingers. "I don't want you. Not in my life and definitely not in my bed."

Sylvia cringed, as if his every word was a physical blow. Her liquid brown eyes glimmered with unshed tears as she turned and ran away.

Chapter 15

Cassie stormed through the front door. She sprinted up the stairs, taking them two at a time. In her hurry, she never noticed Lil on her way down and almost barreled into her.

"Oh my goodness!" Lil exclaimed, visibly startled.

Cassie sidestepped her. "Sorry, didn't see you there," she said as she unlocked her bedroom door. She sensed more than heard Lil follow her inside. *Would she ever have a moment of peace?*

"So how did it go at Asa's?" Lil asked.

Cassie shrugged out of her duster and tossed it on the bed. "Good." She removed her gun belt next. Perhaps seeing her undress would cue Lil to leave.

"Good," Lil repeated with a smile. It was a labored smile, a gossamer guise like a bridal veil revealing more than it ever intended to hide. Something was troubling Lil, Cassie realized, feeling lower than dirt. Here she was trying to get rid of the poor woman when all Lil needed was a friendly ear.

"Is something wrong, Lil?"

Lil wrung her hands together, her nervous gaze edged toward the door as if she were both reluctant and eager to leave. "You didn't happen to run into Sylvia at Asa's did you?"

A bitter taste flooded Cassie's mouth. She struggled to maintain a conversational tone. "No."

"What in the world could be keeping that girl?" Lil bit her bottom lip. "I only sent her for some eggs and sugar. But she's been gone for hours!"

"I wouldn't worry about it."

Lil marched to the door. "Well, I do worry," she grabbed the doorknob. "I'm going to look for her."

"Don't bother."

Lil stopped short. Turning once again to Cassie, she

99

lifted an elegant eyebrow in silent question.

"I saw her on the way back," Cassie said. "She was with Cole."

"Oh," Lil acknowledged softly. "Were they on their way home?"

Cassie managed a tight grin. "They didn't seem in much of a hurry to go anywhere. Except maybe one of them private rooms in that saloon."

Lil blushed. "I see."

Sitting on the edge of the bed, Cassie stretched her arms over her head. She yawned for added emphasis. "I'm beat. Think I'll take a bath and hit the hay."

"But supper's almost ready," Lil said.

"I'm not hungry."

"But Juanita said she made your favorite," Lil insisted.

Cassie smiled. "Which one would that be? According to Juanita, all her dishes are my favorite."

"I'm not quite sure how to pronounce it," Lil confessed with an embarrassed laugh. "But it smells absolutely scrumptious."

"And it no doubt will be," Cassie said. "But I really am beat. Go on and have supper without me. Tell Juanita to save me a plate for later."

With a disappointed look, Lil turned away. "All right," she said, shutting the door softly behind her.

Cassie sagged against the mattress and stared at the ceiling. Try as she might, she couldn't dispel the unsettling memory of Cole and Sylvia in the alley. Her stomach responded with a slow, molasses-like churning, finally settling into a million tiny knots.

To think she almost let him kiss her in a similar fashion. Why, she practically swooned in his arms like a lovesick strumpet.

Cursing, she stomped to the dresser, ripping several drawers open. With no particular item in mind, she delved through their contents, sending a flurry of garments to the floor. She caught a glimpse of herself in the vanity mirror, and abandoned her desultory search. She looked a fright. Her hair was a knotted, wiry mess. A combination of sweat and trail dust matted her unruly curls against her forehead, and her face was smudged with dirt. She was in dire need of a good scrubbing. Though her wounds were healing rather well, she admitted, eyeing the fading, yellow bruise in the corner of her mouth.

Palming her errant curls aside, she inspected her injured temple. Like those dreaded headaches, the ugly gash had all but dissipated. In its wake remained a white, razor-thin scar. After giving her reflection a final assessing look, she grabbed a towel from the commode and hurried down the stairs, looking forward to a long, hot bath. She found Juanita standing by the kitchen door, eavesdropping by the looks of it. Knowing Juanita as well as she did, it came as no surprise. Keeping as quiet as possible, Cassie crept up behind her, and tapped her on the shoulder.

Juanita spun around, her wide, alarmed gaze turning to relief at the sight of Cassie. "*Diosito*, but you scared me."

"Just what do you think you're doing?"

Juanita brought a finger to her lips, motioning for her to keep quiet. "Come," she whispered as she took Cassie's hand.

"Where are we going?" Cassie let Juanita drag her up the stairs.

At the top landing Juanita said, "I do not think they heard us."

"What do you mean 'us'? You were the one eavesdropping," Cassie corrected. "I was on my way to take a bath."

"It is *la bruja*," Juanita said, using her favorite moniker for Sylvia.

Cassie made a face. "Sylvia back so soon?"

"*Sí*, and *señorita* Lil is very angry with her." A mischievous light swirled in Juanita's mocha eyes. "*La bruja* was gone for a very long time, and she did not go to the store like she was supposed to. Instead, she was with the *señor!*"

"I know," Cassie said, feeling an increasing sense of guilt. At the look of surprise Juanita gave her, she elucidated further. "I saw Sylvia and Cole on my way back, and I told Lil. But I never intended to cause any trouble. It's just that Lil was very concerned about Sylvia.

I only wanted to put her mind at ease."

"Why do you worry?" Juanita asked. "*La bruja* does not like us." Scrunching her face with displeasure, she added, "*Señorita* Lil should get rid of that one. She is no good."

"You think Lil's going to fire her?"

"I prayed for that," Juanita cast a disappointed glance heavenward, "but *señorita* Lil is too kind. She sent *la bruja* home for a few days, is all."

Cassie munched on a fingernail. "So Sylvia's gone, then?"

"Not yet." Juanita pointed to the floor. "She is down there saying that she loves the *señor*." She imitated Sylvia's whining voice. "That he promised to marry her."

Cassie's spine stiffened as if pulled taut by an invisible string. "Then I don't understand why Lil's upset. If Cole intends to marry-"

"Bah!" Juanita eyes flared with indignation. "I told you before, the *señor* does not want her. He would never marry her."

Cassie couldn't respond. Her tongue felt glued to her mouth.

Like an endless procession, the image of Cole and Sylvia kissing played over and over in her mind. Making a liar out of Juanita and an utter fool of her.

Chapter 16

Later that evening, Cassie tossed and turned in bed. She was miserably hot, and not a single wisp of air drifted through her open bedroom window. When she rolled onto her side, her muslin chemise stuck to her back. With a scowl, Cassie plucked the moist fabric from her skin like a giant scab. *So much for that refreshing bath she took earlier.*

From far away an owl hooted, joining the cacophony of nocturnal, chirping insects already grating on Cassie's nerves. With a grunt, she rolled out of bed and wiggled into a pair of trousers. Throwing on a clean shirt, she didn't bother buttoning it to the collar; it was much too hot for that. She stomped her boots on, grabbed the oil lamp, and crept downstairs to the front porch.

Taking a seat on the porch swing, she set the lamp on the floor, then rested one foot on the banister. She couldn't help but smile at the conniption Juanita would have if she saw her sitting in such a vulgar manner.

"What are you chuckling about over there by your lonesome?"

The unexpected voice startled Cassie. She swiveled in her seat and skimmed a hand over her hip, in search of a phantom weapon carelessly forgotten in her room.

With a flickering candle in hand, Lil emerged from a shadowed corner. "I'm sorry if I startled you."

"That's all right," Cassie said, taking in Lil's pink, crepe robe and matching nightgown.

Lil placed her candle on the banister. She turned to gaze at the stars, her thick auburn braid swung over her shoulder. "I couldn't sleep," she ventured. "You?"

"Couldn't sleep either."

"Besides, this is the only time Cole and I get to talk," Lil said. "Sometimes he comes home, and sometimes he doesn't. But I wait up for him just the same. He doesn't realize how much I worry about him. But, I do. He's all I got." She turned dark, soulful eyes on Cassie. "Has he told you much about our family?"

No, and I prefer to keep it that way.

"No." Cassie hoped the remote tone of her voice would discourage Lil from reminiscing any further.

No such luck.

"Our folks came over on the wagon trail from Virginia," Lil began.

"I know," Cassie said. "Cole did tell me about your ma passing. I'm sorry."

"I was just a baby, then. I don't even remember her." Lil's voice was laden with guilt.

Cassie wanted to tell her that she shared her pain. That after all these years, her own mother's face was nothing more than a nebulous image, the sound of her voice a distant echo she could no longer recall. But she remained quiet, realizing it was best to keep Lil at a safe distance. Like her brother, the woman had an uncanny knack of burrowing through her defenses, to that soft, fragile pulp inside.

"I know Cole's profession is not the most noble," Lil said, evidently undeterred by Cassie's silence. "But he is a good man."

"There's no such thing." Cassie leaned back in the swing, making it creak. "The way I figure it, nobody is all good or all bad. We're all a little of both. It's just some folks got more of one in them than the other."

"I suppose," Lil said. She crossed her arms and leaned against the post. "Cole was always good with a gun. From the time I was knee-high, I remember him playing with Pa's guns. He was always so..." she frowned, as if searching for the right word, "...comfortable with it."

Using the foot propped on the banister as leverage, Cassie rocked herself slowly, maintaining her silence.

"We settled in this little farming town just south of Tucson," Lil added with a sad smile. "Pa started a pig farm, but it didn't work out. Nothing he ever tried his hand at worked out."

Cassie stopped rocking. "This is rough land."

"It was especially hard on Pa," Lil said, and by the glassy look in her eyes, Cassie could tell she was right back at that pig farm. "He had his hands full with Cole. In school, my brother was always getting into scraps with the other boys. Most were a lot older than he was. A lot bigger, too, but that made no difference to him."

Cassie couldn't keep from asking, "What were the fights about?"

Lil looked away. "We were very poor," she said. "We didn't have money for fancy clothes and such. We had some hand-me-downs from a few kind neighbors. And the reverend in town, Reverend Holloway, also helped us out whenever he could. He used to come by the farm with food and clothes. The other kids would poke fun at Cole and me because we wore rags, and oftentimes went to school barefoot."

Cassie shifted uncomfortably in her chair, at a loss for words.

"And those were the happy years. It got worse after Pa..." Lil fingered the buttons on her robe, "...took his own life."

Cassie met Lil's eyes. "He killed himself?"

Lil nodded. "I was only eight when Pa hung himself in the barn. Cole found him, he'd gotten into another fight and the teacher sent him home." Lil took a shaky breath. "He had to...cut him down."

Cassie's heart convulsed at the revelation. "That's horrible, Lil."

Lil rambled on, as if she'd never heard her. "We didn't have no other kin. It was just me and Cole. Reverend Holloway fixed it so we could stay at this orphanage in Texas. I know he meant well, but I hated it there," she said in a harsher tone. "After a few weeks, Cole ran away, promising he'd be back for me soon as he made enough money to care of me proper. He wrote to me regularly, and I couldn't wait to read his letters. I was so jealous of him, thinking he was out there living this grand adventure. At least, that's what it seemed like at the time."

Lil rubbed her hands up and down her arms. "Now, I only see the hard facts. How he slaved away at those mining camps, before working for the railroad, then as a cowpuncher, a hired hand, whatever he could do to make money. I don't know exactly when he got into what he does now. I reckon it was when I started getting letters fattened with more money than I knew what to do with. It made him a wealthy man." She turned large, tortured eyes on Cassie. "You know, I didn't recognize him when he came for me. Of course, he'd grown, and there was this tall, handsome man in place of my skinny brother. But there was a coldness about him, this hard look in his eyes. It frightened me." She shook herself, as if trying to dispel the memory.

"First thing he did was buy me all the fancy clothes I ever wanted. He swore that as long as he was alive, I'd never want for anything, that we'd never wear rags again. He brought me here and surprised me with this big, fancy place that's all paid for," she lifted her eyes toward the boarding house.

Cassie hadn't expected that. She assumed Lil ran a boarding house because she needed the income. "Why turn it into a boarding house?"

"What was I going to do with an eight bedroom house?" Lil said with a shrug. "I thought Cole would stay with me, but he told me the house was for me. He said if he wanted a house, he could buy his own. I figured a boarding house would be a good idea. It was a way that I could make my own money, so Cole wouldn't have to worry about me all the time. Not like I have to run the boarding house to survive. With Cole's guidance, I've invested a lot of my earnings," she said with a contended smile. "So whenever I want the house all to myself, I just stop taking in boarders, like I did now that you and Juanita are here. But what I really like the most, is my independence.

"Careful," Cassie teased. "You're sounding like a suffragist."

"Reckon I am," Lil said. "Don't see why we should be treated any different on account of our sex."

"Amen to that!"

Lil blushed. She dropped her gaze to her lap and added in a shy voice, "You know, some folks say I'm bound to end up a spinster."

Cassie jerked a shoulder up. "I've been called worse."

"I don't intend to be, though. I had a beau...well he wasn't really my beau, just that...when folks realized who my brother was, it scared off any potential suitors I could've had. But I would like to marry someday."

Cassie snorted with distaste. "What for? So your husband can start running your life and taking over your business? Leaving you at home with the children while he's out frolicking all night?"

"Not all men are like that," Lil said.

Cassie rolled her eyes. "Yes they are. Men are all the same."

"There are plenty of married folks that are happy."

"I'm sure there are," Cassie said with a dry laugh. "Just like there are plenty that ain't. And usually the unhappiest member is the wife."

"I'm sorry that you feel that way, Cassie."

Cassie bit her lower lip. "I'm not," she replied more harshly than she intended.

Lil sighed, then turned her head to inspect the darkness hovering like a black shroud beyond the front yard. "I reckon this is one of those nights Cole won't be coming home."

Cassie followed her line of vision, a part of her disappointed with that fact. "He can take care of himself, Lil."

Lil response with a small nod. Taking her candle, she walked to the door. "You know, I don't think I've ever had such an open conversation with another woman," she said. "I really enjoyed our talk."

Cassie didn't turn to look at her, but she smiled just the same. "Me too."

"Good night, Cassie."

Cassie mumbled a good night as she relaxed in her seat. *Marriage.* She relinquished that silly prospect years ago. Not that she ever considered it a plausible option at any stage of her life. Her father had been fiercely protective of her, and for him, no man was good enough for his daughter. It was he, who instilled in Cassie her distrust of men. He warned her about the lecherous tendencies all men harbor, and the duplicity of their words. He always said a woman had everything to lose and nothing to gain, but a bastard in her belly.

After her father passed on, and she took over the business, she'd discovered even more unappealing qualities about men. They are violent and domineering, too proud to work for a woman, but not to abuse her when they deemed fit. She had only to recall her own difficulties with Raul, not to mention Ike Raines...

Cassie shivered and hugged herself. Don't think about him, she ordered, squeezing her eyes shut, trying to shift her thoughts to more positive things. Like rebuilding her ranch. She could see it in her mind's eye, clear as the Arizona sky. The sprawling L-shaped structure with elaborate wrought iron railings on the front porch, the Spanish tile roof, and parapet walls with brick coping. She would rebuild it just as it was. She must have dozed off in the midst of her musings. That realization hit her when the jangle of spurs startled her awake. Her heart thumped like a frightened jackrabbit, and she sat up.

The soft light from the oil lamp bathed Cole in a golden light as he approached. "Waiting up for me, darlin'?" he asked, a roguish grin lifted one corner of his sensual mouth. "I'm touched."

He removed his hat, smoothed his thick hair with one hand. A few errant strands fell forward to skim his jaw, giving him a deliciously unkempt look. His ivory, silk shirt shimmered in the lamp light, defining every hard line of his torso. With his leather boots and felt pants, he looked every part the gentleman. Except for that gun belt riding low on his hips, the holster secured to one thigh with a rawhide strap. Lil's words flowed through her like warm honey, and a tiny knife twisted in Cassie's heart. He would never wear rags again.

"Hardly," she said, watching him lean a hip against the banister.

He was deliberately crowding her! It was a spacious porch, and she could think of no other reason for him to stand between her splayed legs. Not that she should be sitting like that to begin with. Regardless, if she shifted positions, it was as good as admitting he intimidated her. And she wouldn't give him that satisfaction. She leaned back, lifted her chin to meet his even stare.

"You shouldn't be out here, alone," he said, eyes dropping to the swell of her breasts.

He might as well have touched her, the way her body reacted to his probing gaze. Her breasts tightened, her nipples puckered into painful, tight buds. She considered buttoning her shirt, but a part of her enjoyed teasing him. Let him get a glimpse of what he'll never have.

"But I'm not alone," she said, the sound of her voice pulling his eyes to hers.

"You were in town today."

Cassie lifted a brow. "You spying on me now?"

With a lazy grin that flooded the very core of her with a strange heat, he replied, "Let's just say that you manage to make an impression. Not too many gals ride through town wearing trousers and gun belts." His eyes traced the path from her boots to her shirt. "Not your best bib and tucker, darlin'. What you got against skirts?"

Cassie ignored the taunt. "I telegraphed home."

"Brady?" Cole asked, more in confirmation than in question.

She nodded.

"You going back, then?"

"If he asks me to."

"Hell, woman," Cole plowed a hand through his hair in frustration, "you never learn, do you?"

Cassie gave him a look that could eat through steel. "You trying to make a point?"

"It's not just your life you're risking," he said, his eyes like granite daggers. "Or don't you think about anybody but yourself? What about Juanita? Haven't you put her through enough? Haven't you put us *all* through enough?"

She rose to level her eyes with his. "I never asked for your help. Besides, you never did explain how you just *magically* appeared that night. How did you know?" she demanded. "Or were you a part of it all along?"

"You really think that?"

The disbelief in his voice shamed her. She looked away. "I don't know what to think. All I know is that I can't be hiding out forever, either."

His voice was a feral whisper. "You forget what almost happened to you in that barn?"

The reminder was like a physical blow. She felt as if a phantom mallet had swung into her gut. Keeping her eyes downcast, Cassie couldn't manage a response through her constricted throat.

"Then go," he said, "but keep in mind that this time I won't be around to save your fool hide."

Propelled by a surge of blinding rage, Cassie curled her fist, and struck him with all the force she could muster. She watched as he dabbed blood from one corner of his mouth, the look in his eyes prompted her to step back. But she didn't make it very far. With a menacing calm behind his every movement, he grabbed her and shoved her against the wall. The force of the impact ripped the air from her lungs, and she cringed, anticipating a blow.

Instead, he sank both hands into her hair, and covered her mouth with his own.

Chapter 17

Cassie tried to break away. Caged between Cole's hard body and the wall, she squirmed and twisted her face, trying to escape his bruising kiss. When that didn't work, she sank her teeth into his bottom lip. That only fueled his resolve, because he bit her back just as hard, her pained outcry gurgled in her throat with no means of escape. With a fistful of hair, he held her head in place as he ravaged her mouth. He forced her lips to part, his tongue delving into her mouth, tasting, sucking, robbing her of breath and reason.

Like a dying tempest, Cassie yielded to him. Her entire body ignited with a rapacious yearning she couldn't describe, and could no longer control. She tasted blood, and wondered through the fiery haze clouding her judgment, if it was his or her own. She moaned when his hand slid between the gaps of her buttons to grip her breast. He kneaded it fiercely, tweaked the puckered nipple between two fingers. Liquid fire coursed through her, and she clung to him, returning his kiss with equal fervor.

He tore his lips from hers to trail small biting kisses along her neck. Gripping the shoulders of her shirt, Cole pulled it to her elbows, the buttons lining the front snapped open with little resistance. Cassie felt a soft breeze caress her bare breasts, and a part of her realized if she planned to stop him, she'd better do it now.

But she hurt. Her heated sex pulsated with a crippling ache. When he suckled her tender breasts, she gasped from the sharp jolt of pain and pleasure that spiked through her like a bolt of lightening. Grabbing the crook of her knees, Cole wrapped her legs around his waist, ground his pelvis against hers, making her acutely aware of one glaring fact. He was very aroused.

She struggled then, panic washing over her in cold

111

waves. "Cole..." she whimpered, trying to push him away, "...please...stop."

"Shit," he said.

Cole released her without a moment's hesitation. He stepped back, regarding her curiously, as if he hadn't expected her to stop him.

Slightly dizzy, Cassie fumbled with the buttons on her shirt. She stared at the wooden floor, her cheeks burned, her mouth as dry as cuttlebone. She was mortified, appalled by her wanton behavior. She was no better than Sylvia. She opened her mouth to speak, but Cole brought a finger to her lips.

"Don't," he said.

Unable to maintain his unwavering stare, Cassie turned away. "I'm sorry. I...I shouldn't have hit you."

From behind her, he swore violently, but she pressed on. "We're both mature enough to realize this was a mistake. We let our tempers get the better of us, is all," she rationalized. "Let's just put it behind us, agreed?"

He failed to respond, but she could feel his eyes boring into her back like bullet holes.

"Sure," he finally said, ending the charged silence between them. "Whatever you say."

The cool tone of his voice galled her. With a nod, she swiped a fugitive tear away and slipped through the front door.

****

Cole poured himself a cup of coffee and took a seat at the kitchen table. He was in a foul mood. Lack of sleep and a hangover tended to do that to a man. Taking a sip of his coffee, he winced when the cup touched his bruised lip. *Damn, that woman hit like man, too.* But she was all woman. Last night had proven as much. Cole grinned in spite of himself. The memory of Cassie's firm, strong body sent a bolt of desire spiking through him. He liked how they fit. She was tall enough so he didn't have to bend over to kiss her. It was mighty nice not having to deal with a cramping neck after kissing a woman. Of course, a sore lip was a whole other matter.

He still couldn't figure out why she stopped him. Hell, if he'd ever understand females. They were a contrary lot. It was obvious Cassie wanted him, just as

112

much as he wanted her. Not like she had to worry about her virtue, so he couldn't understand her reluctance.

But something else bothered him, too. The encounter left him wanting more. Yes, he was savagely attracted to her. He wanted her in a way he'd never known before. It was more than her physical assets, bountiful as they were, that attracted him. Cassie had gumption and more grit than many men he'd encountered. She was smart, opinionated, and headstrong. All the attributes that would send most men into hiding for the rest of their lives. Only in her, he found them all the more appealing. *What the hell was wrong with him?*

"Fancy seeing you up so early in the morning," Lil said. She walked into the kitchen with a toothy grin and a spring to her step. She'd always been a morning person. A trait that had skipped him.

Cole turned weary eyes on his sister. "You implying I dally in bed too long?"

"From the looks of you, I'd say you needed to dally in bed a lot longer," she observed as her eyes roamed his face. With a glance at the cup in his hand she asked, "Did you leave me any?"

He gestured toward the stove. "Just made some."

Bringing a spare cup and the blue enamel pot to the table with her, Lil took the empty seat beside him.

"So, you decided to come home after all," she said, filling her own cup.

Cole smiled, and shook his head. She'd always been a worrywart. "Seems that way, don't it?"

"I waited up for you last night."

His smile vanished. "On the porch again? Damn it, Lil, I keep telling you not to do that."

"I was having trouble sleeping." She gave him an innocent look. "Besides, I wasn't alone. Cassie kept me company until I turned in. Was she still out there when you got home?"

"Yeah," he answered, avoiding his sister's curious gaze. "You're both plumb crazy sitting out there in the middle of the night."

With a sigh, Lil tucked a silky strand of auburn hair behind her ear. "Well, it's not like we were there *all* night."

"You shouldn't have been out there at all."

"Oh, you're just a big grump in the morning." Lil ran a playful hand through his tousled hair. Her eyes searched his face, stopped at the corner of his mouth. She reached a hand toward it. "What happened?"

Cole pulled his face away. Not wanting to get into any specifics, he said, "Just a disagreement of sorts."

"I do hope you let the poor fellow walk away with his life intact, yes?"

Oh, she walked away all right. As if nothing had ever happened. "You could say that."

"Honestly, Cole," Lil scolded, "you plan on living like this the rest of your life? Don't you ever think about settling down?"

"What do you suggest?" he asked with a shrug. "That I invest in one of them mail order brides?"

Lil met his teasing gaze with a hard one. "According to Sylvia, you've already promised to marry her."

Blast that woman's lying hide. "That so?"

"Is it true?"

Cole looked at his sister with some surprise. Lil knew him better than that. "What do *you* think?"

Lil let out an exasperated breath. "I'm sorry, Cole. I'm not doubting you. It's just that girl is going to be the death of me. Every time you come back, Sylvia goes plumb loco. Why, I had to send her home yesterday. Told her not to come back until she's sure she can focus on her work, and nothing else."

That brought a smile to Cole's face. He looked heavenward. "Hallelujah!"

"It's not for your benefit." Lil smacked his arm. "It's more for hers. I won't have her making a fool of herself by chasing you all over town."

"Word travels mighty fast around here," Cole remarked.

"I'm not one to gossip, you know that," Lil said. "But I was worried sick about Sylvia yesterday. I sent her to Asa's for some things we needed for supper. It shouldn't have taken her longer than an hour or so. Yet she was gone most of the afternoon. You can imagine how downright scared I was. Cassie returned just as I was on my way to look for Sylvia. She told me not to bother because she saw Sylvia with you at the saloon."

Cole's coffee cup stopped midair. He looked at his sister. "She did, did she?" He wondered exactly how much Cassie saw.

"I don't know what you and Sylvia were doing," Lil said. "And I know it's none of my business, you're a grown man, after all. But you should at least take Sylvia into consideration. Her reputation is at stake."

Cole suppressed a laugh. "You're saying that like she's got one left to salvage."

"I'm serious, Cole."

"So am I."

"But that certainly didn't stop you from taking her to your bed, did it?"

"I didn't take Sylvia to my bed," he clarified. "She crawled in. And quite uninvited if I recall."

Lil shook her head. "And you simply couldn't find it in your generous heart to turn her away."

"I'm a man, Lil," he said. "Not a saint."

"That's what all men say." Lil clucked her tongue with disapproval. "Maybe Cassie's right. Maybe men are all alike."

Well, she had plenty of experience to draw upon, he figured. That fact settled as badly as curdled milk in his stomach. "She drawing that conclusion from her own ample experience, I reckon?"

A smile lifted the corners of Lil's mouth. "You've got a hankering for her," she stated. "A bad one."

"That I do, little sister," he said with a shrug.

"What are you going to do about it?"

Cole wiped all emotion from his face. He curled a hand around his cup, his knuckles bloomed white. He recalled how the previous night culminated. Cassie was right. It was best to put it all behind.

"Nothing," he answered. "Nothing at all."

Chapter 18

From his office window, Sheriff Brady watched Barrington amble down the boardwalk, clearly headed in his direction. The sight of Katherine walking demurely beside her husband blackened his mood. Hissing a curse, he sat at his desk and reached for a fountain pen. He immersed himself in paperwork he'd finished hours earlier and didn't bother looking up when Barrington entered his office.

"Sheriff, my good man," Barrington saluted.

"Amos," Brady said.

"Hello, Sheriff Brady."

The sound of Katherine's voice ebbed the sting from his tone. "Ma'am."

"Seems you're a might busy," Barrington said. "I can come back later."

Brady put his pen down. He looked up from his desk and found it difficult to keep his eyes from straying to the golden-haired beauty at Barrington's side. "That won't be necessary. How can I help you?"

The cattle baron took the only seat available in front of the sheriff's desk. "Well, I had the members meet at my house yesterday, Sheriff."

Ignoring him, Brady rose from his chair. He brought it around his desk and offered it to Katherine. "Ma'am?"

"You're very kind, Sheriff," Katherine said with a nervous glance at her husband. "But I'm fine."

Barrington pushed the chair away with a fleshy knee. "Let her be, Sheriff. She's on her way to the general store anyways. Ain't that right, dear?"

Katherine's eyes met Brady's for the briefest moment. "Yes, that's right."

Brady watched her walk to the door. He admired the gentle sway of her hips, the dignified set of her shoulders.

"Women," Barrington snorted the moment he was

alone with the sheriff, "all they know how to do is spend our hard-earned money."

Brady ignored the remark. "You were saying you met with the members? Even Cyrus?"

"Even Cyrus," Barrington said. "Hell, Sheriff, in difficult times, a businessman puts his personal feelings aside. Now we all agreed that what happened to the Taylor woman was most unfortunate. But, until she's found, we got our ranches to worry about, they're our livelihood. With this drought, somebody needs to be in charge, making sure we're all getting our share of the water. The members took a vote and decided I should take the lead for now. I was honored, of course..." Barrington chuckled and shook his head as if he were the recipient of some grand prize, "...but the other members felt it only made sense on account of how much stock I own."

Though he battled the urge to smack the saucy grin from Barrington's face, Brady managed to smile. "Well, I wouldn't get too comfortable in your new position just yet, Amos. Miss Taylor is coming back very soon."

Barrington's eyebrows rose into his balding hairline. "So you found her?"

"She telegraphed me," Brady said, offering no further explanation.

Barrington laughed. "Well, I'll be damned..." He blotted perspiration from his temple with a silken handkerchief, "...where's she been hiding herself?"

"Can't rightly say."

"So when's she coming home?"

Brady gave him a cool smile. "This is still an open investigation, Amos. You'll understand if I'm not as forthcoming with any information."

"Of course, Sheriff. I just wanted to let the other members know, is all. You know, set their minds at ease."

"You can tell them I'll be escorting her home very soon," Brady said as he shifted his attention back to the papers on his desk.

"Well, that's mighty good to hear." Barrington stuffed the handkerchief back in his pocket. "Hell, I knew she'd turn up sooner or later. I sure am glad she's all right."

Brady dipped his pen in the glass inkwell. "Is there anything else?"

Taking the obvious cue, Barrington rose from his seat. "No, no, that'd be all for today, Sheriff." He put on his hat. "I'll leave you to your work."

"Amos," Brady called, prompting the older man to glance back from the open doorway. "Where's Mitchell? Thought you never came to town without him."

"Oh, he's moved on."

His curiosity piqued, Brady turned his full attention to Barrington, who now seemed a might eager to leave. "Is that so? When?"

"Few days ago," Barrington said with a roll of his shoulder. "I seen it comin' for weeks, now. Mitchell's a restless feller. You know the sort, always fightin' the bit."

"Man like that was bound to get bored in this town," Brady said.

"That he did, Sheriff. You have a good day."

Brady reclaimed his vigilant post at the window. He watched Barrington cross the street and practically knock Katherine over as she exited the post office. *The man treats his wife no better than a dog.* His fist clenched as the two appeared to have a verbal altercation of sorts, which ended in Barrington shoving his wife aside none-too-gently as he entered the post office. The poor woman had to grasp the boardwalk railing to keep from toppling face-first onto the dirt road.

Brady fought the urge to walk over there and beat the daylights out of Barrington. Katherine, ever the lady, was quick to regain her composure. He watched with growing admiration as she straightened her sunbonnet and smoothed her skirts. She smiled, albeit mechanically, at several townsfolk who greeted her. As if she knew he'd been watching her all along, Katherine's eyes strayed to his window. Brady swallowed hard and held her gaze. The genuine smile she gave him brightened her pretty face. He tipped his hat at her in response. His sole comfort lay in the fact that Barrington would soon meet his maker.

Though Cassie Taylor hadn't revealed much other than her location in her telegram, he was certain she would finger Barrington. Once she did, he'd be more than happy to hang the odious, puffed-up swine himself.

Court trial be damned.

Chapter 19

"No, sir. You're mistaken. I added it all up, and I don't get three dollars and fifteen cents," Miss Prudence exclaimed with a shake of her gnarled fist. "I run a business, too, Asa. You're trying to rob me blind."

Sylvia stood in line behind Miss Prudence, a bottle of stomach bitters in her arms. Growing impatient, she glanced at the clock on the opposite wall. Mr. Johnson would be closing soon, but that had never dissuaded Miss Prudence in the past. She would have left the moment she saw the old hag in the store if Ma hadn't needed the stomach bitters.

"Nobody's trying to rob you, Prudence," Mr. Johnson said. "See for yourself." He pushed the order log toward the old woman. "It's all there. Last week, you bought two yards of that pretty lace you like, and you told Marybeth to add it to your account. Now that right there'll run you ten cents a yard. Then you had me order you some of that special cold cream all the way from New York City..."

"Miss Prudence," Sylvia interjected. "I'm in a hurry. Do you mind if I pay for this while you straighten out your account?"

"Stomach bitters, eh?" The old hag's rheumy gaze settled on the bottle Sylvia placed on the countertop. "Your ma still suffering from that indigestion?"

Old busybody. Sylvia forged a sweet smile. "Yes."

"Honestly, Asa," Miss Prudence grumbled, her gaze back on the order log. She ran an arthritic finger down the list. "You sell those tonics that don't do anybody a lick of good."

Mr. Johnson handed Sylvia her purchase in a paper bag. "That'll be a fifty cents."

"Huh!" Miss Prudence snorted. "It's highway robbery in here."

"Now Prudence, I won't stand for that nonsense in

119

front of my customers," he scolded. "How would you like it
if I went to your dress shop and started bellyachin' about
your prices in front of your customers?"

"Oh posh! You don't know the first thing about
running a dress shop."

Anxious to leave, Sylvia placed her money on the
counter between the squabbling pair. "Thank you Mr.
Johnson."

"Sylvia, wait," he called.

Gritting her teeth with annoyance, Sylvia stopped at
the door. "I really need to be going."

"It's won't take long," he said, cramming a large hand
into his front apron pocket. "This is for Miss Taylor.
Would you mind giving it to her?"

Sylvia studied the envelope he handed her, and tried
to keep the giddiness from spilling into her voice. "Of
course not. I'd be delighted."

"The wife and I are leaving tomorrow for San
Francisco," he said. "You remember, Millie, my oldest?"

It was a telegram. Sylvia couldn't believe her luck.
"Yes, I remember Millie," she said unable to rip her eyes
from the envelope.

"She's blessed us with our first grandson."

"Congratulations."

"Miss Taylor's been waiting on that telegram," Mr.
Johnson said. "Both she and Lil dropped by this morning.
But it came through less than an hour ago. With
Marybeth gone for the day, I was going to deliver it after I
closed up." Gesturing behind him, Mr. Johnson gave
Sylvia an exasperated look. "As you can see..." he dropped
his voice to a whisper, "...Miss Prudence is fixin' to keep
me here a spell."

Sylvia gave him a knowing wink. "Don't you worry,
Mr. Johnson. I'll make sure Miss Taylor gets this right
away."

"Oh my," he exclaimed and scratched his head. "I
don't know where my mind is these days. I forgot to log it
in my book." Sylvia watched with mounting horror as he
reached for the telegram again. "I'd plumb forget my own
head if it wasn't attached. Reckon it's all the excitement
about the trip and the baby."

"Nope!" Miss Prudence shouted. The outburst

stopped Mr. Johnson's hand midway. "These numbers just ain't right, Asa. I owe you seventy-five cents. Not a penny more."

"Seventy-five cents?" Mr. Johnson repeated. He turned to glare at the old woman who was scratching off numbers in his book. "Now how do you figure that? And stop mucking around with my log."

Sylvia stuffed the envelope down her skirt pocket. "So you're leaving Marybeth in charge until you get back?"

"What's that? Oh..." Mr. Johnson shook his head, "...yes, that's right. Marybeth will be in charge."

"I like Marybeth," Sylvia said.

He blinked, as if trying to gather his thoughts. "Um...yes...she's a mighty fine gal."

Seeking to keep the man's attention on anything but the telegram, Sylvia continued, "What's your grandson's name?"

Mr. Johnson gave her a brilliant smile, his massive chest swelled even further with pride. "Jake Asa McIntyre."

"You must be very happy."

"Asa!" Miss Prudence bellowed again.

Mr. Johnson closed his eyes, his broad shoulder wilted. "Coming!" he shouted back.

Without another word, Sylvia darted out of the store.

Chapter 20

Anxiously awaiting Brady's response, Cassie made it a point to stop by the post office on a daily basis. And every day, Marybeth Johnson, assuming the postmaster role in her father-in-law's absence, sent her home empty-handed. By week's end, with still no word from the sheriff, Cassie's frustration had turned into a combustible mix of fear, anger, and worry.

"Are you sure it didn't come in before Mr. Johnson left?" Cassie insisted. She gave Marybeth an imploring look. "Maybe he forgot to tell you."

Sitting at the postmaster's desk, Marybeth shook her head. "Asa's a very organized man. I doubt he'd forget to tell me if anything came in. Even if he had, he would've logged it in the book, and I already looked in there."

"Could you just check the log one more time, then?"

With a sigh, Marybeth opened the desk drawer, and produced a leather-bound notebook.

"Here," she said, offering it to Cassie. "See for yourself."

Cassie took her time flipping through the log. *Mr. Johnson was indeed a meticulous man.* A ruler-guided ink line divided every page into two columns: Incoming and Outgoing. She saw her name in the latter, along with the date and time she telegraphed Encanto earlier in the week. She grew increasingly more dejected as she leafed through the rest of the journal, her name glaringly absent from the remainder pages.

She returned the book to Marybeth. "Thanks anyhow."

"I've got an idea," Marybeth said with a snap of her fingers. She took a seat at the telegraph machine.

Cassie watched the young woman work the device. The meaning behind the tapping sounds transmitted through the metal plate lost on Cassie's untrained ears.

"What are you doing?"

Marybeth lifted a finger, signaling her to remain quiet. With a couple of final taps, she reclined in her chair. "It shouldn't take him long to telegraph back."

"Who?" Cassie asked.

Almost immediately, the telegraph came to life, clicking and spewing static like a bellicose infant. Marybeth reached for a sheet of paper and converted the incomprehensible sounds into written word. When the machine quieted, she handed the page to Cassie.

"I wired the postmaster in Encanto," Marybeth said. "Asked him to confirm that he'd gotten your telegram."

Cassie read the short message, despair bubbled in her chest:

received telegraph-delivered to sheriff monday

"I appreciate that, Marybeth," she said, barely recognizing the stricken sound of her own voice. She left the paper on the desktop. "I...um...gotta head back."

Marybeth followed her out to the hitching post. "See you tomorrow?" she asked as Cassie climbed into the saddle of her waiting mount.

"Don't see much point in it. Do you?"

Cassie spurred her horse into a gallop, never giving Marybeth a chance to reply. Arriving at the boarding house, she stabled the palomino and walked toward the front door. Rounding the corner, she saw Sylvia on her way out. The young woman waved a farewell to Lil who waved back from the porch.

When Cassie approached her, Lil explained, "I told Sylvia she could come back tomorrow. On the condition she's on her best behavior, of course."

Cassie refrained from making any comment. Lil had a right to do what she wanted in her own establishment. She was mighty fond of Sylvia, though Cassie couldn't understand why.

Lil turned back to the house and held the door open for Cassie. "So?" she asked, the moment Cassie joined her inside. "Any news?"

Cassie stopped by the stairwell, poised to respond when Juanita emerged from the kitchen.

"*Señorita*! You are back!" she exclaimed, her face glowing with renewed anticipation. "Anything from the

123

sheriff?"

"I was just asking her that," Lil said.

"Nothing," Cassie answered, watching the light fade from Juanita's eyes like water through a sieve.

Hope was a cruel thing.

"Are you sure?" Lil asked.

Cassie nodded. "I even checked the log myself."

"Well, perhaps the sheriff is out of town," Lil suggested. "He probably hasn't received it yet."

"*Si*," Juanita chorused. "That could be."

"He got it, all right!" Cassie shouted, losing her patience. "Marybeth telegraphed the postmaster in Encanto. He wired back confirming that my telegram was delivered to Brady on Monday."

Juanita gasped. "There must be some mistake."

Cassie chewed the tender insides of her mouth, her stomach dropped a grim peg. "There's no mistake," she said as she turned away. "Now, if everyone will just excuse me…"

"But *señorita-*"

From the top of the stairs, Cassie silenced Juanita with a wave of her hand. She marched straight to her room and locked the door. Her troubled thoughts plagued her as she paced at the foot of her bed. Had Raul been right about Brady? Was he really in Barrington's pocket all along? The sheriff had been her sole lifeline. Her one chance to reclaim her life and make Barrington pay for his crimes. She'd been so certain he'd come through for her.

Clearly, her instincts had failed her.

Sitting at the edge of her bed, Cassie raked both hands through her hair. What was she to do now? She certainly wasn't about to spend the rest of her life in hiding like some two-bit outlaw. While the real criminal got to live high on the hog. With balled fists, she punched the mattress beneath her. No. Barrington would pay, all right. She would make him rue the day he slithered into Encanto. He would pay for every insult, every joke at her expense, every vile, filthy rumor he ever spread about her. He would pay for destroying her home, for Paco, and Mario, and Raul. For Juanita, who hid her pain behind a ready smile. But most of all, he would pay for sending that pig to...to...

As if physically assaulted, Cassie flinched with the memory of Ike Raines. She closed her eyes, forced it back while tears spilled down her cheeks. *Damn Amos Barrington to hell.* The hate she harbored for the man was a palpable thing. It pulsated inside of her, threatened to take a life of its own. At that very moment, she swore to destroy Barrington, by any means necessary.

And she knew just the man for the job.

After all, isn't that what men like Cole Mitchell did for a living-stepped in where the law couldn't or wouldn't? Besides, Cole knew more than he was telling. Why? Who was he protecting? She simply had to find a way to get it out of him. The hardest part, of course, would be finding the courage to face him again.

Since their altercation on the porch, she strived to avoid him at all cost. Foolish woman she was, she initially thought that would prove difficult, living under the same roof and all. She couldn't have been more wrong.

Of late, their paths seldom crossed, and when they did, Cole's indifference was downright insulting. It stung her pride he could just saunter by her with nothing more than a hasty tip of his hat. On a couple occasions, he failed to acknowledge her presence entirely, his insouciant gaze skipped over her as if she were an invisible phantom existing in some nether realm.

She reckoned she should be grateful for his reticence. After all, hadn't she been the one to suggest they pretend like nothing every happened? But she wasn't grateful. Not in the least. If anything, she hated him for it.

Cassie spent the rest of the day in her room, emerging only to take her evening bath and share an atypically quiet supper with Juanita and Lil. After helping Juanita with the dishes, she retired again. In her room, she paced, brushed her hair, changed the bed linens, cleaned her gun...just about everything she could think of to mollify her anxiety.

After hearing Juanita and Lil retire for the night, Cassie tried to get some sleep. Changing into her nightgown, she lay in bed. All to no avail. Her beleaguered mind kept sleep at bay.

With a frustrated sigh, Cassie rose and walked to the

window. She stared at the full moon, hanging low in the night sky. From outside her bedroom door, the familiar sound of Cole's heavy footsteps caused her heart to skip a beat.

Now would be a perfect time to talk to him. She bit her lower lip, gathering confidence. Turning to the vanity, she looked at herself in the mirror. She couldn't very well see him dressed only in that. The conceited lout would probably think she was trying to seduce him. She rummaged through the dresser and found a light blue shawl in the bottom drawer. Wrapping it snugly around her shoulders, she slipped into the dark hallway.

Cassie stood in front of Cole's room for some time, staring at the hazy, amber light glowing through the gap at the foot of the door. Taking a deep breath, she finally knocked.

Several moments passed, but she heard no movement from the other side. He couldn't have fallen asleep so soon, could he? She knocked again.

This time, Cole's voice filtered through the closed door. "Not now, Lil."

Cassie debated whether she should identify herself before knocking again. The words wouldn't push past the blasted lump in her throat, so she simply knocked again.

The door swung open. "Damn it, Lil, I said-"

This was a bad idea. The man wasn't the least bit happy about seeing her. A muscle clenched along his jaw, and his eyes hardened like cement drying in the sun as they roamed the length of her.

She struggled to maintain a decorous tone to her voice. "Can I talk to you?"

He regarded her in silence, as if he couldn't decide whether to let her in or slam the door in her face. Cassie braced herself for either outcome. Her fingernails dug into her clammy palms. Then with a shrug, he turned around, but left the door open for her.

With heart pounding, Cassie stepped inside. Yep, this was definitely a bad idea.

"Close the door," Cole said over his shoulder.

She did so and watched him reach for a crystal decanter on the nightstand. He poured some whiskey into a matching tumbler, and tossed it back. Without looking at her, he shrugged out of his shoulder holster, discarded it on the bed next to his duster and gun belt. It was the first time she saw him in a state of undress as he took a seat in the smoking chair. His unbuttoned shirt hung over his broad shoulders. Her eyes slid along the smooth, tanned skin of his chest, down the muscle-corded abdomen, to the light dusting of hair beneath his navel.

"I'm waiting." He rested a booted foot on the opposite knee.

Cassie ripped her wandering eyes from his body. Seeking a safer place for them, she stared at the decanter at his side.

"Mind if I help myself?"

He raised a dark brow. "That ain't no afternoon tea, darlin'."

"You don't say?" she said, pouring herself a small amount in his glass.

She downed the contents in one gulp. Though she felt the liquid singe a hole in her empty stomach, she refused to show any discomfort. Instead, she poured herself another, raised it in salute at his surprised expression, and tossed it back.

He laughed then, a deep, throaty rumble that turned her knees to jelly.

"Hell, woman, you got more crust than an armadillo."

"I've been wondering..." she cleared her scorching throat, "...how much it is that you charge for your services?"

His smile died then, his eyes narrowed into amber fissures. "Don't quite get your meaning."

"You know," Cassie continued, turning her back to him. "How much do you charge to kill a man?"

"Depends on the man."

She faced him. "Pardon?"

He stood and approached her, dwarfing her in the process. "It depends on the man," he repeated. "A powerful man like Barrington, for example, won't come cheap."

She shrugged. "How much?"

"A thousand."

Cassie let out a small, brittle laugh. "You can't be serious."

"Are you?"

"Yes, I am."

He gripped her elbow, his fingers like pincers digging into her skin. "You think killing a man's easy?" He shook her. "Even when he's done you some wrong, it ain't, believe me."

Cassie tried to maneuver her arm free. "I'm sure I'll be able to live with it. I'm not sorry that Raines is dead."

"Neither am I, but that's different."

"No it's not," she said, her eyes watering at the memory. "Barrington sent him, so he might as well have been in that barn himself. I won't feel a damn thing except relief when he's dead."

Cole shoved her away. "What about Brady? Thought you were relying on the law to help you."

"Seems like he's not all that interested in helping me much..." Cassie rolled her eyes, "...since he hasn't even bothered to wire me back. Besides, there's not a lot he can do for me, anyhow. Not like there's any real proof against Barrington, is there?"

Cole matched her challenging stare. "No, there ain't."

"Right, so that doesn't leave me with a whole lot of options."

"Why not just do it yourself?"

Cassie stared at the tip of her bare toes that peeked through the flouncing hem of her nightgown. "I've never killed a man before," she admitted. She could barely recognize the stricken sound of her voice. "I don't know if I can."

"But you got no problem getting somebody else to do it for you."

The sour tone of his voice riled her up. She tossed her shoulders back. "I came here to talk business, Mr. Mitchell. I don't much care what you think of me."

He dragged a chilled gaze along her body. "You got that kind of money lying around?"

"I have enough in the bank to cover that, yes."

"I'll be damned," he said beneath his breath.

"Of course, I-I don't have that kind of money on me now," she stammered. "I'd have to go to the local bank first and request a transfer of funds and-"

"Keep your money, woman," Cole said. "I don't want

it, and I don't need it."

The raptorial look in his eyes gave Cassie pause. Choosing her words carefully, she asked, "Then what?"

He moved in closer. Cassie backpedaled away until her tailbone smacked against the dresser.

"What I've wanted from the moment I laid eyes on you," he answered savagely. "You. In every and any possible way."

She should've been insulted, at the very least outraged by his brazen admission. She wasn't. If anything, she found his blunt manner strangely arousing. Her breath came in choppy bursts as if she'd just run for miles in the open desert. Her heart punched her ribs like an angry prisoner.

She tightened the shawl around her shoulder. "I didn't come here for this."

"Is that so?" He shrugged out of his shirt, the silky material gliding over his muscles like liquid gold. "Then leave, I won't stop you. But if you stay, you're going to spread those sexy thighs for me."

A mixture of fear and excitement surged through Cassie like an icy undertow. She stared at his naked chest, longed to smooth her hands over every chiseled plain, to run her fingers along every band of muscle roping his abdomen. She doubted she'd ever see a finer male specimen again in her lifetime. She choked on the grim realization she wanted this. Wanted *him*. So badly, it physically pained her. Keeping her eyes averted, she unclenched her fist and let the shawl slip through her fingers.

The conceding gesture seemed to surprise him. He observed her a quiet moment. "You better be sure about this, Cassie," he finally said. "I won't stop this time."

She lifted her chin to gaze into those whiskey eyes, seeing nothing but a steadfast resolve staring back at her. "I'm sure."

With tremulous fingers, she reached for the lacy straps of her nightgown, and slid them over each shoulder. The nightgown slipped to her feet in a ruffled whisper. She stood before him wearing only her knee-length drawers. To her surprise, he didn't even glance at her exposed breasts. He just looked deep into her eyes, one finger tracing her clavicle bone.

"You're shaking like a leaf," he observed, running that same finger down the length of her arm. "Are you afraid?"

"Yes," she whispered, her eyes fluttered closed when his lips grazed the sensitive skin behind her ear.

With one hand at the small of her back, he pressed her against him. "Why?" he murmured between kisses.

Cassie couldn't think straight with him nibbling at her neck like that. She squirmed in his arms. "I don't know."

He kissed her then, with surprising tenderness. His mouth moved over hers, his hands cupped the sides of her face. Cassie parted her lips, letting his tongue slip through. She loved how he tasted, traces of tobacco, whiskey and something sweet she couldn't quite place. Her hands skimmed the sides of his lean torso. Her fingers traipsed over the ladder of his oblique muscles. She felt a shudder ripple through him. He moaned into her mouth. Capturing her exploring hand, he jerked it downward.

"Here," he ground against her lips, "touch this." He unbuttoned his fly, letting his engorged member spring free.

Like warm satin on steel.

Cassie stroked him, feeling him grow harder in her palm. *As if that were possible.*

She wanted to look at it, but he kept kissing her, and she couldn't drag her lips away long enough to steal a glance. In her mind, she tried to make a note of his size, knowing it was of crucial importance. Especially for a virgin. A lifetime of breeding livestock and working alongside men made her more knowledgeable about sex than her unmarried counterparts. She winced at her tactile-based estimations. She stroked him harder, feeling the bloated veins, the bulbous head as she tried to assess his length. She was on the verge of outright panic. He would never fit inside of her.

With a groan, he pulled out of her grasp. "I won't be much good to you later if you keep that up."

He ran a hand up her belly, cupped her right breast. She closed her eyes and gasped with the jolt of desire that

Dry Moon

spiked through her when he pinched the sensitive nipple.

"You're so beautiful," he said.

Reaching for her other breast, he gave it the same wonderfully rough treatment. The tone of his voice was genuine as was the admiration she saw in those amber eyes. But men fancied women with soft, rounded bodies, and ample bosoms. Everybody knew that. Her toned, sinewy frame and teardrop breasts were far removed from that ideal.

Tearing her eyes away, she mumbled, "You don't have to say that."

"No man ever told you before?" he asked, sweeping her hair over one shoulder to plant a hot kiss on her neck.

She shook her head, shivers running down the valley of her spine.

"Bloody fools," he purred.

He knelt and trailed hot kisses along her belly. Reaching for her drawers, he pulled them over her hips and to her ankles. He helped her lift one foot, then the other out of them. Cassie's fingers curled around the dresser's edge, she ducked her head, hid her flaming cheeks behind her hair.

Cole ran a hand over her bottom, his fingers dipped into the moisture between her legs. "Nice and wet already," she heard him say, the tone of his voice one of masculine pride. At that very moment, she hated him. Hated her weakness for him.

He lowered his head. Cassie's breath caught in her throat when he parted her slick folds with his tongue. Her entire being ignited with heat like a live stick of dynamite. She felt his tongue dip inside of her, circle the perimeter of her heated opening. Cassie moaned. Lost in a maelstrom of raw desire, she ground her throbbing sex against his mouth. She whimpered in protest when he drew his mouth away, and came up from his knees.

Cupping her chin, Cole rasped, "Look how good you taste," before crushing his mouth against hers.

Cassie savored her own juices in his mouth, intoxicated by the sweet, musky taste. Eager for more, she sucked on his tongue, linking her arms around his neck. This time, his kiss was ravenous, insatiable, and she feared she couldn't satisfy his fraught need. Cole threaded his fingers in her hair, and crushed her against him. Her breasts flattened against his hard chest. Without breaking the kiss, he walked backward, bringing them both onto the bed. He rolled on top of her and nipped a steamy trail along her neck.

Through the sensuous fog clouding her senses, Cassie heard his boots drop with a thud, one after the other, onto the floor. She felt as if her loins were on fire. Her vaginal muscles clenched, pained her in earnest. She moaned into his mouth as he lifted his hips and rid himself of his trousers. Using his knees, Cole nudged her legs apart. Feeling his hardness press against her inexperienced sex, Cassie stiffened, her entire body buzzed with renewed apprehension.

As if sensing her uncertainty, Cole reared back, looking deep into her eyes. A worry line marred his smooth brow. "What's wrong?"

Cassie forced a tiny smile. *He'd find out soon enough.*

"Nothing," she lied, kissing him again. She tried to keep her fears at bay, telling herself it would be fast and painless.

Cole's hands gripped the slim expanse of her waist and traveled upward, cupping her breasts. Cassie arched her back as he dipped his head to suckle her. Her nipples ached; the dull throb between her legs pounded an angry tempo. Her fears all but dissipated, she strained against Cole, seeking release from the glorious torment. His exploring hand moved downward to the sensitive, hooded bud of her desire. He stroked it, using a firm, circular motion.

Cassie gasped. Raw pleasure surged through her like a burning current. Almost painful in its intensity, she succumbed to the sensual fugue his finger invoked. A ragged cry escaped her lips, and she arched her hips in response. He kissed her throat, licking and biting along the way. Then he interlaced his fingers with hers, pinning her hands against the mattress.

Cassie felt him enter her, and she bit back a scream. Lost in a torrent of raw pain, she crunched her eyes shut, gasping against his forceful invasion. Her inner muscles strained to accommodate him, stretched to their limits, the searing pain was unbearable. When he finally reached the veil of her resistance, he went very, very still.

"Cassie," she heard him say after an edgy pause. "Look at me."

She really wanted to. She just couldn't find the courage at the moment. They were still locked together, and she could feel him, deep inside of her, hard and hot.

"Cassie," he repeated, harsher this time. "Look at me."

He was angry with her. She had expected that much. Taking a deep breath, she opened her eyes, and met his turbulent stare.

"You've never done this before, have you?"

It was more a statement of fact than a question.

Cassie swallowed hard and shook her head. The tortured look in his eyes was like a physical assault. She tore her gaze away. "I'm sorry," she whispered. "Are you angry?"

"Just a might," he answered, his voice strained. "You want to stop?"

"No. Don't stop."

Still he didn't move. He remained inside her, rigid, throbbing, but motionless.

"It's going to hurt," he told her, as if he wanted her to change her mind.

Cassie nodded. "I know. It's all right."

He moved again, inching forward until he reached her hymen. Cassie gritted her teeth against the searing pain. She just wanted it over. She hadn't expected it to hurt this much.

"Don't hold back," she pleaded. "It hurts more that way. Do it fast."

With one swift movement, he imbedded himself inside her, tearing through her resistance until he was seated to the hilt. She felt him strengthen his grip on her hands, as if he expected her to push him away. He kissed her, muffling her pained outcry. Hot tears leaked from the corners of her eyes.

"Cole," she cried, tearing her lips free. The burning pain was overwhelming. She couldn't take much more. He seemed to fill her beyond endurance. "I can't. Please. It's too big."

"Shhh…" he murmured as he kissed her face. " Just

relax darlin'. You'll get used to me in a moment." He kissed her neck, nibbled her ear lobe.

Tiny currents of pleasure rippled through Cassie's body. The fact that he seemed to know exactly where and how to kiss her made it that much easier for her to relax. When he reached a hand between their bodies to stroke her most sensitive bud, she sighed with renewed pleasure.

"That's it, honey," Cole crooned, his fingers moved skillfully along her heated cleft. "Just relax."

Cassie felt every bulging vein on his hard member as it dragged against her tender sex. Her flesh softened, her muscles yielded to his invading member, until each thrust hurt a little less, and she wanted more. She bucked her hips, encouraging him to delve deeper. As he did, a strange heated sensation undulated through her entire body.

Cole grabbed the crook of her knees, placed her legs around his waist, and slammed into her. Moaning, Cassie countered his movement, taking all of him, yet somehow feeling as if it wasn't enough. He gave her no quarter. He pounded into her, battered her tender insides, yet still she wanted more.

Cassie ground her sensitive bud against him each time their bodies met, until she reached a fevered pitch. She ran her hands down the length of his back to his tight buttocks. Gripping it, she guided his movements inside her, pushing him harder, deeper. Sweat beaded along her breasts, tiny sparkles shimmering beneath the candlelight.

"Come for me," he whispered, his breath hot against her ear.

Cassie wasn't sure what it was or how to describe it—that moment she shattered from within. She cried out his name as her raw, sated flesh convulsed and contracted, her body quivering with an exquisite, soul-shattering release. Her limbs went numb. She felt weightless, as if she floated above the mattress. Then, she felt Cole thrust completely into her one final time before he withdrew, and spilled himself outside of her.

Chapter 21

It seemed like an eternity passed before Cassie was able to control her labored breathing. Although her heart still hammered a frantic beat. From the corner of her eye, she watched Cole at the commode. He'd left the bed moments after his own release. Without a word.

Anger emanated from him, she could see it in the way he washed her virgin's blood off, and then in the rough manner he donned his pants.

Cassie managed to swallow around the knot in her throat and looked away before he caught her staring. She rose on watery limbs and groped for her nightgown, pulling it over her hips. As the numbing effects of her orgasm dissipated, her lust-sated flesh began to pain her in earnest. The tacky moisture between her thighs conjured images of their lurid encounter. Flames of embarrassment licked her face as she recalled the way he took her, and how she'd hungered for it.

From her peripheral vision, she saw Cole button his pants and rest his hard, lean frame against the dresser.

"You all right?" he asked.

She slipped her drawers over her trembling knees. "Fine."

He stepped toward her. His voice was soft when he spoke. "You're hurt."

"I'm fine," she repeated.

"You're bleeding, damn it." He pulled her to him.

"That's perfectly natural." She tried to keep her temper from flaring. "I'll be fine."

"Christ, you're stubborn as a mule."

He scooped her into his arms and deposited her on the bed as if she weighed no more than a bag of feathers. Cassie scrambled away the moment her bottom hit the mattress. Cole grabbed her shoulders and forced her to lie down.

"Here's what's going to happen." He matched her mutinous stare, but kept his tone conversational. "I'm going to lift your gown and wash your blood off, and you're going to lie there and keep quiet while I do so, got it?"

Cassie muttered a series of expletives. Tired of their constant bickering, and knowing she couldn't very well stop him from doing as he pleased, she slumped against the pillow, staring at some nonexistent point on the ceiling.

Placing the ceramic bowl on the end table, Cole sat beside her. The mattress coils squeaked beneath his weight. Cassie bit her lip when he lifted her nightgown over her hips and bunched it at her waist. He slid a hand between her locked knees to spread her legs. With surprising gentleness, he pressed the cloth against her aching sex, and she sighed when he held it against her sore cavity, the cool dampness assuaging some of the pain. She recalled it was only her blood he washed away. He hadn't spilled his seed inside of her.

He went about the task with an almost clinical detachment, his handsome face a hard mask of concentration. He used a clean towel to dry her off, then carefully rearranged her nightgown to her ankles.

Without meeting his eyes, she stammered, "You didn't...I mean...I should thank you for not..."

"Coming inside of you?" he finished for her.

With burning cheeks, she nodded.

He muttered a response, though she couldn't make out what it was, her attention riveted by his exploring hands. They traversed the length of her legs over her nightgown, smoothed over the expanse of her hips, as if he were sketching a mental map of her form.

"You're thinner," he observed with a frown.

"You didn't seem to mind much when you were screwing me a moment ago."

"Damn," he cursed, and jumped to his feet. "What the hell did you lie for?"

She rolled a shoulder. "I didn't lie."

"You were a virgin!"

"I never said otherwise."

"Of course you didn't," he shook his head. "You only sold yourself like some two-bit whore."

Cassie sat upright against the wooden headboard. "I know what you've heard about me back home, Cole. But it's just gossip, filthy lies started by that filthy pig. My conscious has always been clear. In the end, the truth always comes out."

"So you sacrificed your virginity just to prove a point?" he asked with a smirk.

"Yes. I mean, no."

He sat next to her, giving her a level stare. "Which is it?"

Cassie shrugged. "We made a deal." She stared at him. "I kept my part, and now you have to keep yours. That's all there is to it."

He looked away and leaned forward, resting both forearms on his knees. "Jesus, that night at your barn..."

"Don't think about it," she said, feeling the blood drain from her cheeks. "I don't."

He turned to her. One hand cupped her chin. "You're right," he said. "I'm glad they're both dead."

God, she really wanted him to kiss her. But that would only complicate matters even more. It wasn't like there were any worthwhile feelings between them, anyhow. Aside from a feral lust that had already fogged her better judgment once tonight. As her stomach fluttered with anticipation, she pulled her face away, her reply lodged behind a trapdoor in her throat. Cole's hand lingered midair, as if poised to pull her back. He studied her momentarily before letting it drift to his lap.

"So, what are you going to tell your future husband on your wedding night?"

Cassie wrinkled her nose. "I'm never getting hitched. Husbands are more a nuisance than a necessity."

"You got an answer for everything, don't you?" he commented with a flat grin. "Only problem is most of it's horseshit."

Giving him a venomous look, Cassie scrambled to the opposite side of the bed. She stood, her cheeks burning at the sight of her discarded drawers still on the floor. "I don't care what you think..." she made fast work of scooping them up on her way out, "...now if you'll excuse me, I would like to get some sleep tonight."

"Go ahead, duck tail and run," he said. "It's the only

thing you seem to be any good at."

His hurtful words trailed Cassie into the corridor. Her pride shriveled like a flower left out in the sun when she heard his lock snap in place. She mashed her teeth, fought the urge to pummel his blasted door to pieces. But that's exactly what he wanted her to do, she realized, and she wasn't about to give him that satisfaction. Pulling her shoulders back, she returned to her room, and closed the door softly behind her.

****

Balancing a breakfast tray in one hand, Sylvia used her spare key to enter Cole's room. Evidently in a state of deep sleep, he never even stirred as she approached the bed. Placing the tray on the end table, Sylvia accidentally tipped over the empty decanter. She caught it before it could fall to the floor. A remaining amber rivulet escaped from its uncorked mouth to trail down her hand. Licking whiskey from her fingers, Sylvia watched Cole's sleeping form.

Clad only in his trousers, he lay on his stomach, face buried in the pillow, bed sheets strewn about the mattress as if survivors of a windstorm. She reached a hand to his sleek back and traced the valley of his spine. He shifted slightly, but didn't awaken.

With a contented sigh, Sylvia stepped away from him and went about organizing the room. At the commode, she gathered the used towels, inspecting the bloodstained pair in the washbowl. She turned back to Cole. Her eyes roamed his naked torso for any sign of injury. Finding none, she stepped back to survey the sheets and mattress, her eyes spotting a light blue garment peeking from underneath the bed.

Sylvia reached for it and held it open, giving it a thorough perusal. She brought it to her nose, got a good whiff of the familiar, soapy scent. Her expression blackened. Only one woman she knew smelled like that. Well, like nothing really. Other than plain old soap. Because she seriously doubted Cassie even knew what perfume was, let alone own a bottle. The woman was so unfeminine. *What did Cole see in her?* With a curse, Sylvia threw the shawl on the floor and wiped her boots on it.

She marched to the door, had barely set foot into the hall when she saw Cassie emerge from her bedroom. Sylvia ducked back into Cole's room, a plan forming in her mind. Skewering his slumbering form with a poisonous stare, she unbuttoned her blouse. *She'd show him.* Tiptoeing to the dresser, she looked in the mirror and ran both hands through her neat pompadour. Finally, she walked to the door and waited for the sound of Cassie's footsteps.

Sylvia stepped into the hallway with perfect timing and bumped into Cassie as planned. "Oh! I'm sorry." She made an elaborate play of straightening her blouse. "I didn't see you."

Cassie's wide, startled gaze swept Sylvia from head to toe. "That's all right."

Sylvia smoothed her hair and emitted a nervous chuckle. "I...um, I was bringing Cole his breakfast."

"I'm sure," Cassie mumbled, turning away.

Sylvia scurried after her. "Cassie, wait. I wanted to apologize for my behavior." She increased her pace to match the tall woman's long strides. "I have no excuse for it, and I just hope there are no hard feelings between us."

Cassie responded with a nod of her head as she continued down the hall.

"You won't tell Lil I was in Cole's room, will you?" Sylvia kept her tone remorseful and sniffled for added effect.

Cassie stopped halfway to the stairwell. She turned around, her emerald gaze cold and barren. It matched the tone of her voice. "Whatever's going on with you and Cole is none of my concern."

"I'm not a loose woman," Sylvia said. "He's going to marry me."

With a smile Sylvia didn't buy for a second Cassie said, "Congratulations. You two are made for each other. I'm sure you'll both be very happy."

Watching as Cassie hurried down the stairs, Sylvia smiled in triumph.

Chapter 22

Walking toward the small shed behind the row of bunkhouses, Barrington glanced over his shoulder. He stared into the darkness suspended beneath the moon like a black mantle. Something moved in the shadows, he was sure of it. He squinted, honed his ears, but couldn't make anything out. With a grunt, he continued to his destination.

Soft candlelight illuminated the tiny window of the dilapidated shed. Barrington opened the door and after skimming another cautious glance over his shoulder, stepped inside.

He took a seat at the rectangular wooden table in the center. "Good to see you all healed up,"

"Took long enough," Raines said.

"So, you ready to finish the job, then?" Barrington asked.

Ike gave his boss a smug grin. "More than ready."

Barrington nodded and pushed two sheets of paper across the tabletop. "Here. I think you'll like what they have to say."

Reaching for the papers, Raines read them with a smile stretching his lips. "How'd you get these?"

"Brady said she telegraphed him. So I paid a little visit to the post office. Turns out that ornery postmaster's mighty obligin' for the right price. According to Brady's telegram to her," he gestured to the second paper in Ike's hand, "he's waitin' on a prisoner transport from Yuma before fetchin' her. That gives us time, Ike..." Barrington stressed with a knowing wink, "...all the time we need."

"Shillings, huh?" Ike's oily gaze returned to the first telegram. "Didn't know Mitchell had any kin."

Barrington stood to pace the small room. "Yeah. Got himself some kin, Mitchell does," he said. "So we gotta re-evaluate things now, Ike. We gotta be real smart about this. We can't risk facing Mitchell head on. We gotta be smarter than him. We gotta *outwit* him."

"Maybe you can't risk facing that son of a bitch, but I can," Ike said with a scowl contorting his face. "I ain't scared of the likes of him. I can take him."

"Sure, if ya got a death wish." Barrington laughed at the angry look his range boss gave him. "Hell, ya wouldn't last five seconds in front of Mitchell, Ike, and we both know it."

Raines curled his fists. "I can take him, Boss, you'll see."

The savage conviction in his foreman's voice sobered Barrington. He looked at the angry man. "That's your problem, Ike. You act without thinking. That's why we're in this mess to begin with."

"This mess ain't on account of me." Raines reminded him. "It's on account of that rat *you* can't find. The rat who tipped Mitchell off that night."

Barrington nodded, a smile inched along his face. "Ah, yes, my little rat," he said, turning to look out the window. He laced his hands behind his back. "You know Ike," he said, "smart men like myself, we got something that most folks don't. You know what that is?" Before Raines could reply, he added, "Patience. It's all about patience, Ike. We bide our time, pick our battles, guaranteeing our inevitable success. Even if that means playing dumb for a while."

"I don't get it, Boss." Ike stroked his whiskered chin.

Turning to look at him, Barrington gave Ike a condescending smile. "Of course you don't Ike. That's why I'm the brains here. That's why I need a man like you. You just have to do what I say," he said. "Leave the thinking part to me."

"All right, Boss." Raines rubbed his hands together. "So what do we do now?"

Absorbed in thought, Barrington didn't immediately reply. *No one made a fool of him. No one.* Not even the lethal Cole Mitchell. As the seedlings of a new plan bloomed in his mind, Barrington salivated with anticipation. He couldn't wait to see the look on Mitchell's face after he was done with his precious sister.

"Boss?"

141

Ike's voice pulled Barrington from his reverie. He turned his head to look at him, when the sound of a creaking floorboard from outside the shed door drew his attention. He caught Ike's wide, stunned gaze and gestured for the foreman to remain seated.

"We stick to the plan," Barrington said as if he hadn't heard a thing. He tiptoed toward the door and reached for the knob. "No more loose ends, remember?"

Barrington pulled the door open and smiled at his wife huddled on the ground. "Well, howdy sweetheart," he said. "Come on in." He clamped a fist around Katherine's topknot and dragged her inside before she could run away. "Ya see, Ike," Barrington said, shadowing Katherine as she crawled into a corner of the room. "It's all about being patient. Ya set the trap, and sooner or later, the rat will come get her cheese." He kicked the trembling woman, his boot sinking into her stomach.

Katherine moaned and wrapped both arms around her midsection.

"See the gratitude I get, Ike? After all I done for her." Barrington shook his head as he swiped another boot into his wife's belly.

"A-amos, please..." she wept.

Raines came to stand beside his boss. "Can't trust no female," he said as he lit a cigar. He took a long drag, his sunken cheeks inflated with puffs of smoke. "Wonder how much she knows."

With a hand around Katherine's neck, Barrington forced her to her feet. "I'll find out soon enough."

"I don't know anything, I swear," she said.

"I don't think she's telling the truth, Boss," Raines said.

"You know I've been thinking," Barrington shoved Katherine onto the tabletop, "that it's high time my sweet, devoted wife here started earning her keep." He looked at Ike. "She won't let me fuck her, you know. She locks herself in her room, tells me got a headache, that she's bleeding. She seems to prefer the company of the hands. So I figure, I should start loaning her out."

Laughing, Ike helped Barrington subdue the struggling woman. "Damn, she's stronger than she looks," he said, pinning her wrists above her head.

Barrington grabbed Katherine's flailing legs. "Yeah, she's got some spirit." Taking the cigar from Ike's mouth, he placed the orange, glowing tip inches from her pale flesh. "How much you think I could charge for this fine piece?"

Pursing his lips, Raines gave Katherine a good looking over. "She's a mighty fine woman, Boss. You can make a heap of money off her."

Katherine cringed from the cigar. "Please, Amos," she whimpered. "I won't say anything to anyone, I swear."

"Of course not," Barrington said, running a finger along her cheek. "But you gotta start pulling your weight around here, dear. From now on, you wanna send your family money, wanna buy your sister some fancy get-up, then you gotta earn it."

"Please, let me go! I won't ask you for anything ever again, I swear it," she begged.

Pretending to consider her plea, Barrington asked Ike, "Ya think she means it?"

"Nah," Raines answered.

"Me neither."

Barrington pressed the cigar against her collarbone. The crackling sound of burning flesh filled the room and Katherine screamed. Raines clamped a hand over her mouth.

"Let her holler all she wants," Barrington commanded. Excitement spiked in his gut, his breath quickened. "Ain't nobody gonna help her." He looked at Katherine. "This here's a matrimonial dispute, is all," he said. "Now, hold her good, Ike. I'm gonna let her legs go."

"Don't worry, Boss," Ike said with a chuckle. "I got her."

Barrington walked to the opposite wall and grabbed a cowhide whip hanging from a rusty nail. Returning to the table, he dangled it in front of his wife.

Katherine sobbed, her voice a pitiful high-pitched squeak. "No, please, Amos," she cried. "Please, I'll do anything you want. Anything!"

Leaning over her, Barrington whispered in her ear, "If you think about leaving me or running to Brady, I'll kill your family. Then I'll come for you."

He raised the lash high in the air, and smiled before

bringing it down on his screaming wife.

****

Katherine awakened in pain. It was sharp, sliced through every part of her body like razor confetti. She moaned and tried to turn on her side. But every muscle screamed in protest. Even her fingers hurt. Blinking, she squinted against the brightness in the room. With a start, she realized she didn't know where she was. Last thing she could recall was blacking out in the shed.

The crackling, snapping sound of the whip filled her ears, and she shivered. Bile settled in her throat. With tears fogging her vision, she looked at the bandages on her arms. Someone had taken great care of wrapping the red, angry cuts. Confused, she looked around the room. It was large and sparsely furnished. Nothing but a metal frame bed and a pair of matching oak tables on either side.

With silent alarm, Katherine clutched the sheets against her chest. Her eyes dropped to the unfamiliar nightgown she wore, and a new panic seized her. She tossed the covers aside and struggled to stand just as the bedroom door opened.

"Ma'am?" Sheriff Brady rushed to her side.

Katherine tried to talk, but could scantly manage a scratchy whisper. "Sheriff," she said with relief, her legs wavering beneath her weight.

Grabbing her arms, he steadied her as she sat back down. "It's all right, ma'am."

"Where am I?" she asked, her gaze locked on his.

Brady sat next to her, but kept a proper distance between them. "My house," he explained, watching her intently. "The Pruitt boy showed up here couple days ago with you in the back of his buckboard. He found you in the shed."

Katherine's eyes widened, her head spun. "A couple of days?" she gasped. "I must go home."

Brady curled a hand around her wrist. "You can't go anywhere in the condition you're in, ma'am. Had the doc look you over, and he cleaned you up. But he said you gotta stay off your feet a while."

His hand was warm, strong, yet gentle when he touched her.

"Amos will be looking for me," she said, unable to keep the tears at bay.

Brady's expression hardened. "And I'll be looking for him."

"My family," she whispered to herself as fresh tears pooled in her eyes. "And Jesse? Oh Lord!"

Brady put an arm around her, "He's fine, ma'am," he soothed. "Everything's gonna be just fine."

Katherine rested her head against his chest. "You don't know what my husband's capable of," she wept, her voice muffled by his shirt.

"Then tell me."

She pulled back, looked into those clear blue eyes, feeling as if she could dive into them. "Sheriff..."

He brought a finger to her lips. "It's Logan."

"Logan," she repeated. She liked the sound of it. "It's Katherine."

"Well now, Katherine," he began. He put added emphasis on her name. "Are you hungry?"

She shook her head in denial.

"Thirsty?"

Another shake of her head.

"Now, you must be the cheapest houseguest I ever had," he said as he smoothed her hair from her brow. "But you gotta eat something, just the same."

Katherine watched his eyes darken, turn a deep indigo as they roamed her face. She suddenly recalled her bruises. Had the whip disfigured her? She buried her face in her hands.

Brady pulled them away. "Don't," he said. "You have a burn on your collarbone, and a few cuts on your left cheek." A vein throbbed beneath the smooth skin of his temple. "Doc says it was from the whip, but they should heal proper."

Her eyes fell. "What about the ones on my body?"

"Some will," Brady paused a moment, "some won't."

Fearing her strength would fail her, Katherine wilted against his chest. "Oh, God."

Brady ran a hand through her hair. "Shh. Don't worry, you're still the prettiest gal I ever did see."

With a smile, she pulled her head back and sniffled when she met his eyes. "Thank you. But what are you still doing here? Didn't you have to escort Miss Taylor home?"

"I am. I was waiting until you woke up. Wanted to make sure you were okay."

"But isn't she expecting you?"

He nodded. "I telegraphed her again. Told her to wait for me."

Katherine sighed with relief. "Oh, thank goodness." Turning her face away, she shook her head. "This is so very humiliating." She wrung her hands in her lap. "I am so sorry, Sh-Logan. I don't want to be a burden to you."

Cupping her chin, Brady urged her to look at him. "You could never be a burden to me, Katherine." He ran the pad of his thumb along the line of her jaw.

With a smile, Katherine leaned forward and planted a chaste kiss on his cheek. It was smooth, as if he'd recently shaved. "Thank you."

"You can thank me by telling me all you know," he said. "It's the only way you can help your family and yourself. You do realize that, don't you?"

Katherine tore her gaze away. "Amos is gone, isn't he?" she asked, though she already knew the answer.

"Yeah, right after he got done with you," Brady confirmed with audible scorn. "I went to see him after Jesse brought you here, and a couple of the hands told me. Said they won't be expecting him back for a few weeks. I won't lie..." reaching for her face, he forced her to look at him, "...I wasn't aiming to arrest him, neither. I was fixin' to make buzzard food of him."

"That's not the wisest thing you could do."

"No," he agreed. "But it's what he deserves."

She watched him. "When are you leaving to fetch Miss Taylor?"

He frowned. "Why?"

"Will you take me with you?" she asked with some trepidation, a part of her feared his response.

"If that's what you want," he said with a broad smile.

Katherine placed a hand over his. "It is."

Chapter 23

"This is the second time, Lil!" Cole shouted, dropping his breakfast tray in the sink with a loud clang. "I don't want that woman in my room."

"Pipe down," Lil admonished. "You'll wake the whole house up." She pumped water into the sink. "Besides, you said yourself all Sylvia does is leave you breakfast and cleans up for you, right? She doesn't even wake you."

"That's not the point," Cole said.

"I know." Turning her head at the sound of the kitchen door opening, she dropped her voice to a whisper when Cassie walked in. "Don't worry, I'll have a talk with Sylvia soon as she comes in today."

Cole watched Cassie pour a cup of coffee at the pot-bellied stove, admiring the way her apple bottom filled out the trousers she wore.

"Good morning," Lil greeted her cheerfully.

Glancing at Lil, Cassie muttered a flat, "Morning."

"Mornin'," Cole echoed, not surprised when she failed to respond, much less look in his direction.

It had been this way since the night she'd stormed out of his room. Though he couldn't figure out why. If anything, he's the one who should be madder than a peeled rattler. She lied to him. Hell, she even sold herself like a whore, only so he could discover that she was a virgin. And damn if he didn't relish the fact that she was, he inwardly admitted, not wanting to delve into the reasons as to why he did either. But like it or not, she was going to have to talk to him eventually. They still had to work out the specifics of their *agreement.*

"You're up early," Lil said.

Cassie nodded. "I'm gonna ride out for a spell."

Cole looked out the kitchen window. "Looks like rain," he observed, gesturing to the dark clouds gathering in the sky.

"Yes." Lil said as she wiped her hands with a kitchen towel. "Lord knows it's due time."

Drinking the last of her coffee, Cassie rinsed her cup in the sink. "I won't be long," she said and walked out of the kitchen without a backward glance.

Cole went after her. Grabbing her arm, he stopped her before she could reach the front door. He forced her to face him. "We gotta talk."

Jerking her arm free, Cassie proceeded to walk away. "What about?"

"What about?" he repeated as he reached for her again. This time he tightened his hold. "You forget our arrangement?"

Cassie glared at him. "No, I haven't. Now kindly let go."

Grabbing her other arm, he dragged her against him. "Damn it, woman," he said. "Then stop walking around here like I wronged you." He didn't know whether to strangle her or kiss her silly. He settled for shaking her. "*You* came to *me*, Cassie, not the other way around. I didn't force you to do anything you didn't want to do."

"*Señorita*," Juanita interrupted, her voice heavy with concern as she descended the stairs. "Is everything all right?"

Annoyed at the intrusion, Cole let Cassie go. "Just dandy."

"Yes," Cassie said, rubbing her arms. "Everything's fine, Juanita."

With a baleful look directed at Cole, Juanita assumed a protective stance next to Cassie. "It did not look *dandy* from what I could see," she said, both hands on her ample hips.

"It's fine, Juanita, really," Cassie said.

Apparently unconvinced, Juanita moved even closer to Cassie. "You almost forgot your riding gloves, *señorita*." She held them out.

"Thank you." Cassie took the gloves, pulling them on.

Cole realized Juanita wasn't about to leave Cassie's side. In fact, both women stood with arms crossed, stabbing him with their angry stares. It was evident they were both waiting for him to leave. That was all right by him. Cole knew when to bide his time. With a shake of his

148

head, he stalked down the hall.

****

Answering the front door, Cole gave Miss Prudence his best smile. "Why Miss Prudence, looking lovely as ever I see."

The old woman chuckled and pinched his arm. "Oh you do go on." Her thin nose sniffed the air. "Something smells mighty good."

"Would you like to join us for some lunch?" Cole asked, leading her into the dining room.

At the table, Lil looked up from her plate. "There's plenty for everyone."

"Don't mind if I do," Miss Prudence said. She rubbed her hands in anticipation, her eyes scanning the assorted plates on the table.

Cole pulled a chair out for the elderly woman. "Ma'am."

Miss Prudence took the seat he offered and waved a greeting to Juanita seated across the way. "Been some time since you been round these parts, Cole."

"Yes, Ma'am," he said, taking his seat.

Lil stood up. "What would you like to eat?"

"Oh, just pile on a little of everything," Miss Prudence answered.

Lil disappeared through the kitchen door and returned moments later with a plate of mash potatoes, baked chicken, and corn-on-the-cob. The old woman reached for it. Wasting no time, she dug into the food and moaned with delight. "This is delicious."

"Yes," Lil said as she reclaimed her own seat. "Sylvia's been outdoing herself these days."

"Well, this is some fine cooking," Miss Prudence said around a bite of chicken. "You're mighty lucky to have that girl around."

Wanna bet?

The warning look Lil directed Cole's way stopped him from voicing the thought.

"And just where is Sylvia hiding herself?" Miss Prudence asked as she looked around the room. "I want to congratulate her on her fine cooking."

Lil took a sip of her coffee. "You just missed her. She went to Asa's."

"Oh my goodness!" Miss Prudence exclaimed. Her fork slipped from her hand and landed on the plate with a loud *clang*. Rummaging through her reticule, she pulled out a small, white envelope.

"This is for Miss Taylor," she said, handing it to Lil. "I just happened to be at the post office when it came in today. Marybeth was mighty anxious that Miss Taylor get it pronto. I told her I wouldn't mind stopping by to give it to her myself."

Juanita snatched the envelope from Lil's palm. Ripping it open, she extracted the letter inside. "It is from Sheriff Brady," she cried, her voice elated. She clutched the paper against her heart. "He is coming for her!"

"Let me see that." Cole had to pry the paper from Juanita's fingers. Confused by what he read, he frowned and stared at his sister.

"What?" Lil asked at his continued silence. "What is it Cole?"

He handed her the telegram. "See for yourself."

"I don't understand," Lil said after reading the inscribed message. "According to this, the sheriff's already telegraphed Cassie before."

Miss Prudence chuckled and took a bite of corn with her two remaining front teeth. "Did Sylvia forget to give that telegram to Miss Taylor?"

Cole clenched his jaw. His gut seemed to fold over on itself. "Pardon?" he asked.

The elderly woman paused to swallow a mouthful of food. "Asa gave Sylvia a telegram for Miss Taylor the night before he left."

Juanita gasped, her eyes rounded as she glanced from Cole to Lil. "I knew Sheriff Brady was a good man."

The hand Lil placed on Cole's arm was colder than a dead snake. "Are you sure, Miss Prudence?" she asked.

"Of course I'm sure, I was there when he gave it to her," the old woman said. She smacked her fork against the tabletop. "What's all the fuss for? I'm sure it just slipped the girl's mind. She was mighty anxious to tend to her ma that night."

Pushing her chair back, Juanita pounded a fist on the table. "She did not forget!" she yelled and stormed out of the room.

Miss Prudence gaped at Lil. "Landsakes, what is wrong with that child?"

"Nothing, Miss Prudence," Cole said, exchanging a knowing look with his sister. "Nothing's wrong with her."

With a shrug, Miss Prudence polished off the remainder of her plate. After a double serving of apple pie and coffee, with plenty of milk and sugar, she departed. But not before taking some extra slices of apple pie home with her.

Alone with his sister in the dining room, Cole said, "Sylvia's been a busy bee."

"I can't believe how stupid I've been." Lil shook her head.

Cole pushed his chair back and walked to the open side window. With a wary eye on the black clouds rushing along the sky, he lit a cheroot and took a couple of drags. Smoking usually calmed his nerves. At the moment, it wasn't having the desired effect. If anything, his heart seemed to accelerate with each puff. "Not just you, Lil."

As if she were a permanent fixture, Lil remained seated at the table. "I never thought Sylvia would do something like this." She cradled her head in her hands. "We all knew how important that telegram was to Cassie. She saw how dreadfully worried Cassie was thinking the sheriff had all but abandoned her!"

"I know." *When he got his hands on Sylvia...*

"*Señores,*" Juanita said quietly. She stepped into the room, her face downcast, shoulders slumped. "Please forgive my rude behavior."

"You have nothing to apologize for," Lil said, rising from the table. "I am the one who's sorry. I should've kept a better eye on Sylvia. I should've realized-"

"None of that, Lil," Cole interjected. "There's no way you could've known what Sylvia was up to."

"I always say that one is no good!" Juanita said. "But nobody listens to me."

From outside, the vibrating roll of distant thunder drew Cole's attention to the window.

"*Mi patrona* is still not back," Juanita said to him. "I hope she is okay."

Cole looked at her. "Did she say how long she'd be?"

Biting her lower lip, Juanita shook her head. "No,

151

señor. But she told me she would stay on the main trail."

Lil nodded. "It's the only way she knows."

"I'll fetch her," he said just as the front door opened.

Cole watched as Sylvia walked into the dining room, humming a tune. It took all his willpower to keep his hands at his sides.

"My goodness!" she exclaimed, directing her gaze to Cole. "Looks like the sky's gonna fall out there."

The sweet smile Sylvia gave him threatened to cleave the string hold he had on his temper. As if sensing his duress, Lil placed a supporting hand on his arm.

"Hello, Sylvia," she said.

Sylvia looked all around, as if she'd just realized she was the center of attention. "Why's everyone looking at me like that?" Blood drained from her face. "What's wrong?"

Cole moved toward her. But Juanita beat him to it. Pushing him out of the way, she marched up to Sylvia, and without a word, slapped her across the face.

Chapter 24

From beneath the brim of her hat, Cassie glanced heavenward, not liking what she saw one bit. What had begun as a haphazard litter of disgruntled clouds had banded into an ominous, cohesive unit, like an invading army holding the entire sky prisoner. Grappling with her turbulent emotions and thoughts about Cole, she'd failed to notice them. She'd also strayed from the trail, riding through the dried gulley and into the adjoining canyon. With the sun obscured behind the moat of clouds in the sky, she couldn't even guess as to what time it was. But she knew she should start heading back and pronto. She kneed the palomino to circle the buttes, when a sudden clap of thunder caused the animal to take off in a frenzy.

Cassie took a firmer grip on the reins. "Easy," she crooned. "Easy."

She managed to control the horse and slowed its pace to an even canter. Breaking through a clearing at the end of the canyon, she stopped and scanned the area for the beaten path of the main trail. Thunder reverberated all around her like a gurgling giant. The horse neighed and snorted, shifting restlessly.

"Easy," she repeated, running a soothing hand down its golden neck.

Digging in her heels, she urged the palomino to continue. The road was a few feet away when a gunshot rang out from the buttes above. The horse reared. Cassie struggled to control the panicked animal and remain seated. She squeezed her thighs against its muscular sides, to avoid landing on the rocks. Another bullet ripped through the air, taking her hat with it. The palomino jerked in response. Startled, Cassie countered the animal's movement, and lost her seating. She landed on the ground with a grunt and scurried behind a nearby boulder. With her chest heaving, she watched her horse gallop away.

Cassie stayed low and drew her gun. The rock took the onslaught of shots coming in rapid succession. The continuous incoming fire prevented Cassie from shooting back. She could only cringe and choke on rock dust as bullets whizzed overhead, chipping the boulder like a sculptor gone mad.

Without warning, a hand reached over the boulder and dragged Cassie from her hiding spot into the open. Coughing, she blinked dust from her eyes, as something cold and hard pressed against her temple.

"Drop yer iron."

Cassie stilled. She gaped at her attacker, her blood congealed in her veins with sickening recognition.

"I said drop yer iron." Raines jammed the barrel of his gun against her head.

Cassie's weapon slipped from her limp fingers.

"What's the matter?" Ike asked with a sneer. "Seen a ghost, have ya?" Laughing, he pushed her in front of him. "Move!"

In stunned silence, Cassie walked ahead, the initial shock of seeing Ike Raines, still very much alive, dissipating like water on a skillet.

Ike poked the gun into her spine. "Up there!"

Gritting her teeth, Cassie turned toward the rock-lined trail he indicated. He was leading her to the highest butte she realized with mute horror.

"Mighty quiet, aint'cha?" he taunted behind her. "Betcha thought you was rid of me, ain't that right?"

Curling her fists, Cassie ignored the remark as she trekked up a jagged ridge.

"Ain't that right?" he repeated, tapping the back of her head with his gun.

Wincing, Cassie asked, "Where're you taking me?"

He laughed. "Betcha thought Mitchell did me in, huh?" he said without answering her question. "But you was wrong. I just been laying low, waitin' for the right time. I been trailin' you all mornin'," he said. "Stupid bitch, so busy daydreamin' ya didn't even notice me."

A blistering rage festered in her belly. Cassie felt her limbs tingle with it, like a sudden fever. At one time, she had thought death preferable to a fate suffered at his hands. Now, she realized she didn't want to die. Not here. Not like this. He wouldn't get the best of her, she swore inwardly. Not this time.

"Shoulda seen the look on yer face when you saw me," he said with another throaty chuckle. "Can't wait to see that same look on Mitchell's face. Lousy son-of-a-bitch. Got me a score to settle with him."

Cassie's heart lurched, rattled like an empty can in her ears. "Reckon you're gonna be waiting awhile, because I don't know where he is."

"Aww, now ain't that sweet?" Rained mocked. "You're trying to protect him." Grabbing her elbow, he spun her around to face him. "Well it ain't gonna do ya no good, 'cos I got the jump on the both of you. I been watching you two these past couple of days. I know he's with you. You ain't as smart as you thought, after all, huh? Boss don't like no loose ends, so I gotta set things right." His voice softened to a sickly whisper. "But don't worry, poppet, we're gonna have ourselves some fun first." He sniffed the air around her like a breeding stag. "I got us a nice little cave up on that butte, there. Made it all homey for ya, too."

Cassie recoiled from his putrid breath. "Only a fool does another man's dirty work for him."

He wasn't even listening to her, she realized. He was far too busy looking her over. He licked his lips with lewd anticipation. Before she could turn her face away, he crushed his mouth against hers. Gagging on his intruding tongue, Cassie bit down on it.

He reared back. "Forgot you like to bite." He spat a wad of pink spittle on the ground. Then, swinging his arm, he struck her cheek with the back of his hand.

The blow staggered Cassie, but she managed to stand her ground. Her single-minded determination not to cower before him provided a reserve of unbounded strength. Thrusting her shoulders back, she gingerly wiped blood from her mouth. "You hit like a girl, Ike."

Raines grabbed between her legs. "You'll see soon enough how much of a girl I am." With a grunt, he shoved her back. "Now, git movin'!"

Cassie took extra care along the rocky terrain. The increasing winds slapped her hair into her eyes, hampering her precarious ascent. Raines shadowed her every step. He jammed his pistol into her back whenever she stumbled or slowed to catch her breath. In the sky, lightening-charged clouds roared and flickered with an inner phosphorescent light like a swarm of fireflies.

As she crested the top ridge, Cassie slowed to survey the butte above. It angled downward, with a massive protruding ledge that hung over her like a bedrock awning. "It's too steep," she said.

Raines glanced upward and commanded, "Just climb!"

Swallowing hard, Cassie slid a glance over the side of the butte. Jagged, red cliff folds peppered with jutting cacti-some well over six feet tall with thorns to match-led the way to the canyon's base. Not a viable escape route at all.

"I said climb!" Ike shouted, aiming his gun at her.

"I'm going!" she yelled back.

Using both arms, Cassie hoisted herself onto the cliff top. Bile simmered in the back of her throat when she spotted the cave Ike alluded to at the far end. It wasn't really a cave. More a juncture created by two rock formations that toppled over one another eons ago. Looking over her shoulder, she saw Raines clear the ledge. For once, he wasn't right behind her. This was her only chance. With a moan, she dropped to one knee.

"What are you doing?" Raines said. He approached her slowly. "Git up!"

Moaning even louder, Cassie massaged her ankle. "I think I hurt my leg coming up."

"Quit yer bellyachin'!" He reached a hand for her.

Cassie spun around, throwing a fistful of gritty earth in his face.

"Agh!" Ike yelled.

He raised both hands to his face and rubbed his eyes. Cassie seized the only chance she had. Using all her weight, she rushed forward and tackled him. Her head slammed into his gut.

Ike screamed and landed on his back, his weapon flew into the air, landing on the ground. While he groaned and rolled onto his side, Cassie made a dash for it.

"You bitch!"

Clutching his midsection, Ike stood, tears streaming

a white trail down his sullied face. Cassie jumped out of his reach as he blindly pawed the air in search of her, and without a second thought, she fired the gun.

The shot staggered Raines, jolted him backward like a marionette on a string. Cassie watched as blood seeped from his wounded shoulder, blooming a crimson petal on his shirt. Ike gaped at her. Shock registered in his face as he stumbled back and disappeared over the rim.

Cassie raced to the ledge.

"Help me, please!" Ike begged her.

He gripped the edge with both hands, his wiry frame dangling like a shoot in the wind. Realizing he no longer posed a threat, Cassie threw the gun over the side. It smashed into the serrated rocks below.

"Oh God, no!" he cried with terror in his eyes. "Don't leave me here, please! I'll do anything you want. Just please don't leave me here!"

Unmoved by his pitiful wailing, Cassie just stared at him. Oddly enough, she felt no sense of triumph, no gloating vindication. She felt nothing at all.

Raines clawed at the earth, trying to maintain his precarious grip on the rim. He only succeeded in stressing the overhanging bedrock supporting his weight, until it finally gave way, and crumbled like a cookie in his fingers. His body plummeted to the ground with limbs flailing, his tortured scream echoed in the canyon long after he'd hit the bottom.

Chapter 25

Barrington closed his umbrella, stomped his wet boots on the porch floor. He looked heavenward, watched the black clouds scurrying across the sky. Thunder roared and vibrated around him. A drought buster, he thought with a wide, contented grin. Setting his valise on the ground, he knocked on the front door of the boarding house.

Moments later, a young woman answered. "Can I help you?"

Barrington stared at her. *Yeah, this was Mitchell's kin, all right.* The family resemblance was most uncanny. Down to them odd-colored eyes.

"Pardon me, ma'am," he said. "Are you Miss Mitchell? I was told you run this boarding house?"

"Oh, yes. But I'm sorry, I'm not taking any boarders at the moment." She pointed behind him. "There's a hotel just up the main road."

"Oh, well, you see the stagecoach dropped me off here and err…" He looked out at the rain, "…it'd be mighty obliging of you to let me stay here on the porch 'til the rain tapers off some. Then I'll head on over to the hotel."

Barrington could tell by the way she looked him over she was trying to ascertain how much of a threat he posed. He gave her as warm a smile as he could muster. "I'll just have a seat there," he suggested, gesturing to the porch swing. "I won't bother you none, ma'am. You won't even know I'm here."

From inside the house came another feminine voice. One Barrington recognized.

"*Señorita* Lil, the coffee is ready."

"I'll be right there, Juanita."

Lil Mitchell and Juanita Gomez, all alone in this big house. Just as he'd anticipated. *Yes sir, things were going as planned.* Still smiling, he reached a hand in his pocket and drew his gun. He watched the terror contort Lil's features. She blanched and opened her mouth as if to scream.

Barrington clamped a hand over it. "Uh-uh, none of that nonsense." He turned her around and placed the gun to her head. "Come on, inside we go," he said, kicking the door shut behind him.

"*Señorita*, the coffee is getti-"

Juanita's sentence died in a gasp when her eyes settled on Barrington and Lil in the entryway. "Barrington!" she exclaimed.

"Howdy there, Juanita," he chuckled. "Mighty obligin' of ya, but no coffee for me right now."

Juanita crossed herself *"Madre Santa."*

"That's right," Barrington shoved Lil at the praying Juanita, "ya both better start saying yer prayers."

Huddled into a corner with Juanita, Lil asked, "You're Amos Barrington?"

Barrington gave her a smug grin. "That's right, girlie."

He fired a warning shot into the ceiling. Both women screamed and hugged each other as they backed against the wall.

"That's so you both know I ain't playing around," Barrington said. "Now, move!" he roared, shoving his captives into the parlor.

With hands interlaced, Juanita and Lil stood shoulder-to-shoulder by the couch. "Please do not hurt us," Juanita cried.

"Do not hurt us!" Barrington mocked in a high-pitched voice. He threw his bag at Lil's feet. "Open it," he ordered. "Take out what's inside."

Lil did as he commanded, producing several feet of rope from the bag.

"Now sit," he said.

"What are you going to do with us?" Lil asked as she sat on the couch.

Barrington chose not to reply. No sense gettin' the women all riled up over their inevitable fates. 'Sides, female hysterics was something he'd rather avoid. "You..." he pointed his gun at Juanita, "...tie her up. I want her hands behind her back and her ankles tied nice and tight. I'm gonna be checkin'."

With tears brimming in her eyes, Juanita went about restraining Lil. "Please, *señor*. Just leave us alone."

"Quit yer blubberin'," he snapped.

Barrington ordered Juanita to sit on the couch the moment she was finished with Lil. Keeping his gun carefully trained on them, he grabbed more rope from his valise. After tying Juanita's hands and ankles, he proceeded to loop the rope several times around both women, binding them together from the waist up like Siamese twins.

Barrington stepped back and admired the hogtied women. He walked to the front window and cracked it open. Using his gun, he held the curtain aside. "Now we just wait here all quiet-like 'til my partner arrives," he told them, his eyes on the torrential downpour outside.

With a smile, he left the window and sauntered back to check on his detainees. He took a seat in the upholstered settee across from them. Propping his boots on the center table, he smiled at the poisonous stares they directed his way. "I love the sound of falling rain," he said to no one in particular. "It's a beautiful thing."

"You're a cowardly pig," Lil said with a curled upper lip.

Ignoring the insult, Barrington laced his hands behind his neck. He was just getting comfortable when he heard footsteps on the front porch. Winking at both women, he stood up. "That should be my partner, now!"

Juanita buried her head in Lil's shoulder. "*Diosito!* We are going to die!"

From the window, Barrington aimed his gun at her. "Shut yer trap you stupid cow."

He waited until Juanita settled down, then glanced outside. Barrington didn't part the curtains this time. He didn't really have to. The diaphanous lace material allowed him to make out the shape standing on the front porch with little trouble. "Son of a bitch!"

Barrington swiveled on his heel, glared at the bound, grim-faced women. Their eyes so big and round and wet he couldn't stand looking at them. Clamping his eyes shut, he pinched the space between them. *What the hell was Brady doing here?* With chest heaving, he grit his teeth as the first knock sounded at the front door. Ain't no sense panicking. That would be foolish. He had to think. *Think, Amos, think.*

The second knock, more persistent than the first, made him open his eyes. Turning back to the window, he surveyed the entire front yard and caught a glimpse of his wife peeking from the side of the barn. *Backstabbing bitch.* He wasn't gonna rot in no stinkin' jail. No sir. He'd rather die than face that unsavory future.

His mind made up, Barrington stepped back and repositioned himself, aimed his gun at the window. He had the sheriff's head in perfect range when Lil hollered at the top of her lungs, "He's got a gun!"

His cover blown, Barrington shot off a couple of rounds, not certain as to whom or what he'd hit. He dropped to his belly when the room exploded in a flurry of return fire. Screaming, Juanita and Lil threw themselves face-first to the floor.

During an abrupt ceasefire, Barrington yelled out the window, "How ya doin', Brady? I see you brought my sweet wife with you. You ain't been listenin' to none of her wild stories now, have ya?"

"It's over, Amos!" The sheriff's voice thundered from outside. "Come on out."

Crawling on his stomach, Barrington reached the women. He stood, and forced them to their feet. "Git to the window!"

It took a moment for Juanita and Lil to find their balance. When they did, they hopped ahead of him like competitors at a sack race.

"You want their blood on your hands?" Barrington yelled, shoving the curtains aside to flaunt his hostages.

After a brief pause, the sheriff said, "You let them go, Amos. You're only making things worse for yourself."

Barrington shielded himself behind the women. "We're doing things my way from now on, Brady. You come anywhere near this house, and I'll pump them both full of lead, *comprende?*"

Another silence ensued. "All right, Amos," Brady finally said. "We do things your way."

"Damn right you are." Barrington pulled the women from the window. "Ladies," he said, shoving them onto the

161

floor, "start making yourselves comfortable, 'cos we're gonna be spendin' a lot more time together."

Chapter 26

"Cassie!"

Standing like a sentinel at the cliff's edge, Cassie turned her head to the sound of the distraught voice calling her name. Relief washed over her at the sight of Cole approaching from the opposite side of the butte. He expertly guided his bay horse over the treacherous landscape.

"Over here!" she shouted, waving an arm in the air.

Raising a gloved hand, Cole signaled her to wait for him.

Cassie acknowledged the request with a return wave and turned her attention back over the ridge.

Moments later, she felt him come up behind her. "You all right?"

Cassie nodded, unable to tear her eyes from the broken body at the bottom of the canyon. "That's Ike Raines."

"Raines?" Cole repeated, following her line of sight. "Thought he was dead."

"He is now," she said with no emotion.

Cole's eyes searched her face. A scowl marred his features when they settled on her injured lip. "I heard a scream. Did he hurt you?"

"He ambushed me by the gulley and forced me up here," she said. "I shot him."

"Good riddance."

"It was a clean shot to the shoulder. I only wounded him." Cassie swallowed, the invisible weight pressing against her chest lifted with every word. "I let him fall."

Cole placed a comforting hand on her shoulder. "You did what you had to do."

"I felt nothing," she blurted, her voice strained, tortured. "He was hanging there, begging for help. Crying something awful. I just watched him, even after he

163

smashed into them rocks. I still felt...nothing."

"Some folks would beg to differ," Cole said. "Some say that's the strongest form of hate there is."

"And what do you say?" she asked, a part of her feared the answer.

Reaching out a hand, Cole wiped some dirt from her face. "I'm the least fit to judge anybody, Cassie. After all Raines did to you, I'd say you let him off easy. You got a good heart. What happened here today won't change that."

A phantom knot swelled in her throat. Cassie swallowed it down, staring at Cole with tears blurring his handsome visage. She feared she was coming apart, like a ball of yarn at the mercy of an angry tailor. "Thank you."

Cole nodded and stood silently beside her, as if he understood her moral bedlam. Cassie couldn't help but wonder if he too grappled with his conscious the first time he took a man's life. But she had the acumen not to voice it. Some things were better left unsaid.

Glancing upward, Cassie watched as lightening streaked a venous path across the sky.

"You ain't dressed proper for that gully washer coming," Cole shouted over the roar of thunder that followed.

Unlike Cole, who wisely opted for a rain slicker in place of his customary duster, Cassie was clad only in a linen shirt and trousers.

"Guess not."

"Come on."

Grabbing her arm, Cole led the way to the only suitable shelter around. He left her at the cave's v-shaped aperture just as the downpour commenced. Rain fell from the sky in perforated sheets, gusting winds propelled it across the ground, drumming a hollow staccato against the parched earth.

"Gotta see to my horse. Stay here, I'll be back," Cole said.

Pulling the slicker's hood over his head, she watched him disappear through the rain. Alone, Cassie glanced around the makeshift cave. It wasn't very deep, but it would do. On the ground, small rocks circled a stacked tepee of dry wood, leaves, and twigs. Remnants of Ike's plan to make the cave 'homey' she concluded, swallowing a sudden vinegary taste in her mouth. She wasn't about to let that stop her from taking advantage of the provisions he left behind. By the time Cole returned, Cassie was actively stoking a warm campfire.

He dropped his saddle to the ground and shrugged out of his wet slicker, revealing the bedroll he shielded underneath. "What happened to your horse?"

Sitting on the ground Indian-style, Cassie glanced up at him. "Got spooked during the ambush."

"That's a hell of a fire," he observed, sitting beside her.

Cassie blushed at the admiration in his voice. "Found some dry wood and such around," she said, opting to leave out the part about Raines.

"Soon as the storm passes, we should head back. You'll ride with me."

"What are you doing here, Cole?" she asked.

He studied her. Cassie watched his Adam's apple bob as he swallowed.

"Well?" she insisted, hedging at his uncomfortable silence.

Reaching into his hip pocket, Cole withdrew two folded sheets of paper. He perused each one, as if considering which to give her.

"Here."

Frowning, Cassie read then re-read the handwritten telegram. Each time she grew even more mystified.

problem came up. can't make it before week's close. remember my prior warning.—L. Brady

She stared at Cole, a question parted her lips.

Recognizing her intent, Cole brought a palm in the air. "Hold your horses, darlin', I'll answer your questions soon enough," he handed her the other letter, "reckon that's the one you never got."

Nibbling on her bottom lip, Cassie read the second message.

awaiting prisoner transport from yuma. will come for you right after.

no later than wednesday.—L. Brady

p.s. important! do not travel alone! wait for me.

She noted the date at the top of the Western Union

form. "He telegraphed me soon after he received mine," she said. Relief swirled in her gut. "That can't be. Lil and I stopped by the post office that morning and-"

"It came later." Cole placed a hand on her shoulder. "Marybeth had gone home by then. Asa was going to deliver it. But he got tied up at the store. The next morning, he was on a train to California."

Cassie shook her head. "But he would've left it at the post office for Marybeth."

"Yeah, he would've," Cole agreed with a smirk. "But since Sylvia was at the store that night, he gave it to her instead. She's had it ever since."

Feeling winded and somewhat dizzy, Cassie managed to hold his steady gaze. Mincing each word, she said, "And why, pray tell, did she decide to hand it over to you now?"

Running a hand through his hair, Cole let out a deep breath and recounted the day's events. Cassie laughed when he described how Juanita had slapped Sylvia. Especially when Lil, emboldened by Juanita's act, proceeded to slap Sylvia a second time. She was sorry to have missed that. Cole further said that Lil, utilizing the ruse of telling Sylvia's ma on her, eventually reduced the young woman to tears. In exchange for their secrecy, Sylvia confessed all her scheming. Even fessed up to her uninvited visits to his room, and how she tricked Cassie into believing they were anything but.

Cassie's cheeks suffused with heat over that final revelation. She kept her eyes on the fire, too embarrassed to look at him. "So after all that, I reckon Sylvia's out of a job?"

"That's right," he confirmed. He added to her discomfort by clarifying one final fact. "That time you saw us by the saloon," he began, scooting closer to her, "Sylvia led me out there on the pretext that she needed my help. She caught me by surprise, is all. I never expected her to kiss me."

Still not looking at him, Cassie fingered a loose thread on the seam of her trousers. "You don't owe me any explanations."

"Is that so?"

She detected an edge in his tone, unsure as to its source. "Yes."

Grabbing her face with both hands, Cole forced her to look at him. "Dammit," he cursed. "It bothered you to see us kissing, didn't it?" He gave her a hard shake. "Didn't it?"

Cassie tried to pull away. "No."

"It would bother me to see you kissing some other man. A hell of a lot!" He shook her. "Hell, I'd probably throttle you, and I ain't too proud to admit it."

"Stop it." Cassie closed her eyes.

He sank both hands into her hair, tilted her head back. "No. Look at me."

God, but she'd never met such a persistent man before! Opening her eyes, she glared pure venom at him.

"Why can't you just leave me alone?" she said, using all her strength to break free. She edged away, put as much space between them as she could. "Ever since I met you, I feel as if I don't know who I am anymore. You've taken over my life...I..." Cassie shook her head and rubbed her arms, "...I hate these things you make me feel!"

"Yeah?" He reached for her again, dragged her against him. "Well, I hate that I can't get you out of my head, that I keep wanting the taste of you in my mouth, that I find myself worrying about your fool hide all the time." He let out a deep-winded breath. "Hell, woman," his voice softened, he sounded like a man defeated, "I love you."

The admission stunned her. But no more than her reaction to it. She felt giddy. Her stomach did a series of somersaults. Her heart drummed a frantic melody in her chest. For the first time in her life, she felt truly, and completely, happy.

"Yes, it bothered me," she confessed with a half-smile. "I wanted to hit you. I wanted to pull every stringy blond hair out of Sylvia's head." She palmed his cheek, felt the bristly whiskers along his jaw. "Kiss me, Cole."

With a groan, he complied. Cassie parted her lips, allowing his tongue to slip through. She sucked on it, deepening the kiss. Her roaming hands molded his shirt to the muscular contours of his torso. Cole dragged his lips down her chin, sucked a steamy trail along her neck. With adroit fingers, he undid the buttons of her shirt, and

Karyna Da Rosa

pulled it over her shoulders. He relieved her of her
chemise and pants next, and pushed her onto her back.
Straddling her waist, he stared down at her, tossing his
own shirt by the wayside.

"You're so beautiful," he said.

Emboldened by his admiring gaze, Cassie unfastened
his pants. Grinning wickedly, he lifted his hips so she
could pull them over his legs. Her eyes rounded at the
sight of his swollen member jutting forward proudly. She
marveled at its girth and length as a delicious, pulsating
ache settled at the source of her sex.

"I want you inside of me," she said in a ragged
breath.

Cole kissed her hard then and lowered himself over
her. He nipped his way to her breasts, sucking on each
pebbly nipple. Whimpering, Cassie arched her hips
against his, seeking release from that dull throb paining
her womanly core in earnest now. Bending her knees, she
opened for him, gasping when he buried his shaft to the
hilt with one hard thrust.

"Does it hurt?" he asked, becoming perfectly still.

"Yessss," she purred. Kneading his backside, she
urged him to continue as she spread her legs farther. "It
hurts so good."

A feral grin curved his lips. He pulled out of her, then
pushed back in, hard and deep, prompting another yelp
from her. "You like that?"

Cassie clenched her inner muscles around his thick
member to show him just how much. "Mm-hmm."

"You're going to be the death of me," he ground
against her mouth.

He increased the rhythm then. Gripping her
buttocks, he pivoted her hips and plunged harder, faster,
deeper. Cassie writhed against him lost in a maelstrom of
pleasure-pain. Her fingernails scraped the earth.

Their frenzied coupling intensified, and they strained
against one another, seeking mutual release. A deep
groan escaped him, followed by a ragged "Oh God," and
she found herself smiling with womanly pride. Her climax
began as a feather-like tickling sensation in her groin,
rippling outward like a stone skipping water. Then her
entire body spasmed, her legs turned to jelly. She

exploded, shattered like broken glass as wave after wave of pleasure surged through her.

She was still in the throes of the after tremors when she heard Cole groan her name, felt him push into her one last time, and spill himself inside her depths.

Collapsing on her, he murmured in her ear moments later, "Sorry."

"It's okay," she whispered, running a lazy hand through his hair.

Cole drew back and lay on his side. "I'm sorry."

Turning her head, Cassie gave him a languid smile. "You already said that."

"I was irresponsible."

"We both were," she corrected.

His expression grew serious. "If we did just make a baby, I won't leave you."

Cassie's heart dropped through a pothole in her chest. She sat up, groped for her clothes. "You're not beholden to me, Cole."

"Hey, hey," he said, drawing her back to him. "I didn't mean it like that. Baby or no baby, I'm not fixin' to leave you anytime soon."

Cassie curled against his chest and breathed the smell of him. She smiled with contentment. "When did you know you loved me?"

"Can't rightly say," he answered. "But I can't recall ever feelin' any different since the first moment I looked at you."

A giggle escaped her. "I didn't think you liked me much."

"Nah, just thought you were a might ornery is all."

Cassie pulled away and looked him square in the eye. "How did you know Ike was coming that night, Cole? Why won't you tell me?"

"Hell, woman," he cursed, as he flopped onto his back. "Just let it alone."

"I can't. Not now that I know Brady's willing to help. You have to tell me, please."

Resting an arm over his brow, Cole let out a deep breath. "Barrington's wife came to get me that night. She overheard him talking about it few days prior. She didn't think he was serious until she saw Ike ride out to your spread."

"His wife?" Cassie echoed with disbelief. "But she barely knows me. Why would she want to help me? If anything, she should be siding with Barrington."

Propping himself up on both elbows Cole said, "I don't think she sides with him on much of anything. She's smart enough not to let it show. She's a good woman. Got a good heart, too."

Cassie smoothed her hair back. "Folks say she married Barrington for his money."

"Well they only got it half-right," Cole said with a crooked smile. "I don't think Katherine had much of a choice in the matter. Her ma's awful sick, and Barrington pays for all her medical needs. But he's a mean old cuss with her. Got her scared of her own shadow."

"That poor woman," Cassie said.

"I gave her my word I wouldn't rat her out," he added with a grave look.

Cassie nodded with acknowledgement. "Don't worry, I won't either. By warning you that night, she saved my life and Juanita's. Besides, she's got enough of a cross to bear married to that pig."

"That's for sure."

Cassie slid a glance to the cave's opening. Although the winds had abated, the rain had not. It poured in a steady stream, covering the entryway like a beaded curtain.

"Reckon we won't be leaving 'til morning," she said.

Rolling on top of her, Cole wedged himself between her legs. He buried his face in the crook of her neck. "Gives us plenty of time," he murmured between nibbles.

Giggling, Cassie squirmed against him as goose bumps sprouted all over her skin. "Don't you have to wait?"

He nipped an earlobe. "For what?"

"Before you can...you know..." she gasped when his mouth covered her right breast, "...get ready again?"

He bucked his hips against hers, and she felt that he was more than just ready. "I think I can manage. You?"

"Oh, I think I can even outlast you," she teased, parting her thighs with wanton abandon.

He surprised her by rolling them both over so she

ended up on top of him.

"Then I'm gonna have to let you start doing some of the work."

Tugging on her bottom lip, Cassie looked down at him with uncertainty. She didn't really know what to do. "But-"

He cut her off with a kiss. "Don't worry," he said, guiding her onto him. "I'll teach you."

Cassie whimpered as she took him in, feeling every inch of his engorged shaft drag against her sex. He moved his hips up, starting a rhythm for her to follow.

Before long, she showed him she was a most apt pupil indeed...

Chapter 27

The evening deluge ebbed to a steady drizzle by morning. In its wake, the slippery, muddy mess of a trail hampered the bay horse's progress, already fettered by the double load on its back.

In the saddle behind Cole, Cassie sighed with audible relief. "We're almost there."

Cole nodded as he steered the mount along a steep incline. Peering over his shoulder, Cassie could see the back of the boarding house come into view. As they neared, a cold, clammy hand wrap around her heart.

"Is that-"

"-Brady and Katherine," Cole finished for her, his voice low.

"Mr. Mitchell!" Katherine cried. She ran toward them as they dismounted with the sheriff right behind her.

"What's going on?" Cole asked Brady.

"He knows," Katherine cut in, looking at Cole. "I-I told Logan everything my husband did. I'm not afraid anymore."

Cassie watched Brady put a protective arm around Barrington's wife. "Amos is inside," he said, addressing Cole. "He's got the womenfolk."

Cassie's blood stilled in her veins. She looked at the boarding house. "Oh my God."

"He make any demands, yet?" Cole asked.

"A horse and cash." Brady pursed his lips with disgust. "But he's alone. Ain't seen no sign of Raines anywhere."

"Raines is dead," Cassie said, drawing all eyes to her.

Brady and Katherine exchanged glances. "One less thing to worry about then," the sheriff said.

"Barrington ain't leavin' that house alive," Cole vowed.

Rage had Cassie's heart in a crazy dance. It smacked

against her ribs, leaped into her throat. She bolted to the front of the house. "You pig!" she shouted. "You filthy coward, come on out!"

Cole lunged for her. With both hands on her shoulders, he dragged her away and shoved her against the side of the house. "Stop it!" he demanded. "You plumb lost your mind? You're gonna get yourself killed!"

"He's right, ma'am," the sheriff said. "And you're putting all of us in jeopardy."

Barrington's mocking voice drifted like morning mist along the front yard. "Got yourself some company there, eh, Brady?"

His ensuing chortle turned Cassie's stomach. "I want him dead."

"Then let me deal with him," Cole said. "I can't do that if I gotta worry about your fool hide!"

"I'll stay with her," Katherine offered. She assumed a protective stance beside Cassie. "We won't get in your way."

Cole regarded Katherine for a moment. Then with an acknowledging nod, he let Cassie go.

"You got a plan?" Brady asked Cole.

"Yeah," he said and gestured for the sheriff to follow him.

With mounting irritation, Cassie watch Cole lead Brady far out of hearing range.

"What do you think they're planning?" Katherine asked.

"I don't know."

"The cellar out back," Katherine dropped her voice, "does it lead into the kitchen?"

Cassie looked at her. "Pardon?"

Reaching beneath her petticoats, Katherine produced a small revolver. "I got it from Logan's house."

Cassie noted the look of fierce determination in Katherine's golden eyes. "Yeah, it does," she said. "But it's too risky, and I don't have my gun."

"That's okay," Katherine nodded. "You can still help me."

Cassie glanced at Cole. Both he and the sheriff were engaged in deep discussion, their backs to her. They'd never notice if she and Katherine snuck to the back of the house. Not if they were quick about it.

"I don't know..."

"This is our only chance," Katherine said. "Please, I can't do this alone. I need your help."

Turning her head, Cassie looked at her. "You any good with guns?"

Katherine gave her a wide, knowing smile. "Very."

Cassie hid her reserve behind a blank mask. Katherine had no reason to lie to her. After all, she'd be risking not just Cassie's life, but her own by doing that. Besides, the woman was responsible for saving her life, and Cassie figured she owed her as much.

With a nod, she said, "Okay."

****

Sitting on the couch, Barrington crammed a second oversized piece of pie into his mouth.

"This is some mighty fine apple pie," he said as he licked his right hand, currently doubling as a utensil. He glanced down at the women prostrate at his feet. "You sure you two don't want none?"

"How're we supposed to eat it?" Lil shot back. "We're tied up!"

Barrington shrugged and reached for a second helping. "Women," he mouthed between bites. "Nothin' a man does is ever good enough for 'em."

He was poised to scoop yet another handful of apple filling into his mouth when the kitchen door opened.

"Barrington, let them go," Cassie ordered.

She walked into the room with an armed Katherine, who much to Cassie's relief, didn't cower one bit in the presence of her husband. She wondered how good of a shot Katherine really was.

"Why, hello there, sweetheart," Barrington said in a syrupy tone. His mordant gaze shifted from his wife's face to the pistol in her hand. "Come to join our little shindig, have ya?"

"It's over, Amos," Katherine said.

Digging the barrel of his gun into Lil's head, Barrington snarled, "*I* say when it's over."

"Please, Amos," Cassie said. Seeing Lil and Juanita at Barrington's mercy was more than she could bear. "Please, let them go."

Barrington shook his head. "Oh, now ya wanna be neighborly."

"Let them go, Amos," Katherine repeated, her voice never faltered.

Barrington turned scornful eyes on his wife. "And just what are you gonna do?" he challenged. "You gonna shoot me? Who's gonna pay for your ma's medicines, then, huh? And your sister's schoolin'?"

"I'll work," she said, cocking the gun.

Throwing his head back, Barrington bellowed with laughter, his fleshy shoulders jiggled like cow teats. "Work? You know how expensive it is to keep your ma in that hospital? Ain't no work gonna pay you that much money. Not even if you earn it flat on your back!"

"I'll manage," Katherine said

"I'll manage!" he mimicked. "You stupid cow, you ain't got the guts to—"

The front door flew open, banged against the wall as Cole and Brady rushed in with weapons drawn.

"Let them go, Amos," the sheriff ordered. "Don't make things any worse for yourself."

Barrington rose from the couch. He dragged Juanita and Lil with him, his gun still pressed against the latter's temple. "Ain't that precious?" Barrington's lips curled with a feral grin. "Gonna save the womenfolk, are ya?"

Cassie looked at Cole, who had yet to glance her way since bursting through the door. He stood with his gun drawn, poised, calm, and eerily silent. A cold dread filled her as her eyes followed the invisible line from the barrel of his gun to Barrington's head. He didn't have a clear shot. Lil and Juanita, but more so Lil, stood in the bullet's trajectory.

Barrington seemed to realize this, as well. Ducking behind Lil, he taunted, "Go ahead, take your shot, Mitchell. Maybe the bullet will go all the way through your sister and get to me."

"Just shoot him," Lil screamed at her brother. "Don't worry about me."

"Cole," Cassie said, her breath catching in her throat. "No."

Still, he didn't look at her. He stared only in Barrington's direction. A muscle rolled along the hard line of his jaw, and for one terrible moment, Cassie feared he'd take the shot.

Instead, he lowered his weapon.

"Just turn yourself over, Amos," Katherine said.

"You shut yer trap. No-good slut," Barrington growled. "Now you're shacking up with the sheriff, are ya?" Laughing, he added, "You think I should tell Brady how I had to break you in on our wedding night?"

"You're a poor excuse of a man, Amos," she said, more like a statement-of-fact than an insult.

This seemed to anger Barrington in earnest. His beefy, reddened face jutted over Lil's shoulder, his flaring nostrils reminded Cassie of a charging bull. "Ya done it now, you know that don't you?" he shouted at his wife. "Now your ma's gonna pay the price for your whoring, you lazy, ungrateful bit-"

Without warning and with her serene composure unperturbed, Katherine pulled the trigger.

The unexpected shot jarred Cassie. A scream caught in her throat as she watched Juanita and Lil roll onto the floor with almost coordinated precision. With his human shield lost, Barrington now stood alone, exposed. He stared at his wife in an odd, perplexed way. His massive body jerked once, twice, as he stumbled backward and fell to the floor. A steady flow of blood oozed from a hole between his eyebrows.

Still reeling from the shock, Cassie could only stare as Katherine approached Barrington's lifeless body.

"I'll manage," she told her husband, as if he could still hear her. "I'll manage just fine."

Chapter 28

Standing on the front porch, Cassie watched the undertaker's wagon rattle down the beaten dirt path. Tilting her head, she glanced at a sudden break in the storm clouds. Misty rain shimmered like gold dust in the ensuing sunlight.

With an arm around her, Cole said, "That was a fool thing you did."

"I've already told you it wasn't her idea," Katherine said, seated at the porch swing with the sheriff.

With a smile, Brady patted Katherine's hand. "I need to find me a better hiding spot for my guns," he said. There was no anger in his voice as he tucked a golden lock of hair behind Katherine's ear.

Cassie looked from the couple to Juanita who had yet to utter a single word. Her friend sat next to Lil on the top step. Cassie's heart ached for her. It must pain Juanita to see the sheriff and Katherine together. She wished she could say something to bring the smile back to Juanita's face.

"Fool or not, I'm grateful," Lil said.

To Cassie's surprise, Juanita rose and approached Katherine. "You saved my life, *señora*. I thank you."

"You're welcome, Juanita." Katherine's cheeks bloomed with color. "I know we never really talked much, but I hope we can change that. I think we can be good friends."

Juanita nodded, slid a shy glance at Brady. "The sheriff is a good man. You will both be very happy."

"Why, thank you. That's mighty kind of you," Brady said to her.

Cassie rested her head on Cole's shoulder, breathing-after what felt like an eternity-a sigh of relief.

"Reckon we can go home now." Brady spoke to no one in particular.

Cassie bit her lower lip. Home? She still had to face the daunting task of rebuilding hers. Not to mention Cole. After all, Encanto wasn't *his* home. Did he love her enough to start a new life with her?

Beside her, she felt the change in Cole. He stiffened, dropped his arm from her shoulder. She gazed up at him and found her answer in the chilled bottom of those whiskey eyes. Like a bird shot in mid-flight, her heart plummeted to the pit of her stomach.

Blinking back tears, Cassie looked at the sheriff. "When are you planning on returning to Encanto?"

"We're leaving first thing tomorrow," Katherine answered for him.

Fearing she'd lose the remainder of her threadbare composure if she looked at Cole again, Cassie turned to Juanita. "Come," she said. "We got ourselves some packing to do."

Juanita followed Cassie to the front door. "Oh, *señorita*, I am so happy. I feel like this is a dream." She clapped her hands. "We are finally going home!"

Before Cassie could reach the handle, Cole grabbed her, and pulled her into his arms. "Damn your fool pride, woman. I told you I love you, and I ain't letting you go."

He kissed her long and hard. Cassie could hear the collective chuckles and whispers of the spectators on the porch, but she didn't care. She kissed Cole back with equal fervor, curling her fingers into his hair until everyone and everything around her seemed to disappear.

Breaking the kiss and mindless of the audience hanging on her every word, she said, "I love you, too."

He smiled. "Reckon we both got some packin' to do, then."

Cassie's heart skipped a beat. "You're coming with me?"

"Gotta make an honest woman outta you," he said. "Can't rightly be livin' in sin now, can we?"

"Well, my reputation *is* at stake," she added with a wink. Twining both arms around his neck, she reclaimed his lips.

About the author...

Having grown up in sunny south Florida, Karyna DaRosa currently resides in New Jersey. She makes it a point to travel home regularly, particularly during the winter months. A self-proclaimed history buff and voracious reader of all genres, she admits a weakness for romance novels, and it wasn't long before she started writing her own.

In fact, she penned her first historical romance in the fifth grade. Alas, despite her lofty dreams, it was not a best seller. Though it did serve to cement her love of the craft, and she's continued writing ever since.

Karyna is a member of the Romance Writers of America, as well as the RWA NJ Chapter. She is currently working on her next novel.

Visit Karyna's official web site to find out more about the author and her books: www.karyna-online.com. Karyna can also be found on MySpace at: www.myspace.com/kayscribe.

Printed in the United States
100315LV00001B/146/A

9 781601 540355